Death in Persia

THE
SEAGULL
LIBRARY OF
GERMAN
LITERATURE

ANNEMARIE SCHWARZENBACH

Death in Persia

TRANSLATED BY LUCY JONES

LONDON NEW YORK CALCUTTA

GOETHE
INSTITUT

This publication was supported by a grant from the Goethe-Institut India

swiss arts council
prohelvetia

he original English publication of this book was supported by a grant from
Pro Helvetia, Swiss Arts Council

Seagull Books, 2021

Originally published as Annemarie Schwarzenbach, *Tod in Persien*
© Lenos Verlag, Basel, 1998

First published in English translation by Seagull Books, 2013
English translation © Lucy Jones, 2012

ISBN 978 0 8574 2 823 3

British Library Cataloguing-in-Publication Data
A catalogue record for this book is available
from the British Library

Typeset by Seagull Books, Calcutta, India

Printed and bound by Hyam Enterprises, Calcutta, India

✷ CONTENTS

Wim Wender's film *Wings of Desire* (1987) portrays a city of isolated people whose inner monologues can only be heard by angels. The post-war, black-and-white Berlin backdrop reflects an unnamed melancholy, tinged by the sadness of one particular angel, played by Bruno Ganz, unable to be seen or touched by the woman he's fallen in love with, a trapeze artist played by Hanna Schygulla.

However, the angel decides to relinquish his ethereal existence to join the object of his desire on earth—and he literally falls from the sky to enjoy a human life with her. Technicolor triumphs over black and white, there is a close-up of his blood-spattered, smiling face, and we see a naked Schygulla sitting with her back to us on the bed, suffused in warm skin tones as she too changes to colour. Ganz has the expression of one who knows he has made the right decision.

Death in Persia plays in a similar space between the real and ethereal worlds, between heaven and earth, life and death: trance-like, feverish fragments make up Schwarzenbach's prose, written at different periods and framed by a story of unattainable love. The angel finds a way to reach the woman he longs for in *Wings of Desire*, but the narrator in *Death In Persia*, Schwarzenbach herself, is stymied by various impediments—a hospital confinement, an injured leg, a difficult itinerary across forbidding terrain—and cannot reach her lover, the Turkish Jalé. In a different form of segregation, social circumstances forbid that the two women show intimacy. And finally, Jalé's father forbids her any contact with the outside world. Schwarzenbach uses the device of the angel to shed some light on her protagonist's state of mind. But the figure is far from being a guardian—he is a foreign angel who first fights with her, then reprimands her for expecting salvation. No paternal laying on of hands here, nor the desire of Wender's angel but merely cryptic advice. When Schwarzenbach expresses the hope that his touch might relieve her terrible fear, his reply is indifferent: 'You cannot move,' said the angel pleasantly, 'you are utterly helpless and exposed to the angels of this land, who are terrible creatures. Do not have false hope. Even my decision to fight for you means nothing so far.'

Unlike the protagonist, this angel is at home in the vast landscape that she finds so inhospitable—Asia. Even water does not represent life, but death—fish float upended in the mountain streams. In her characterization of the angel, Schwarzenbach pours all her fear of the alien, which was not from a lack of travelling experience but, more likely, a reflection of her psychological frailty at the time she wrote *Death in Persia*. Not the physical constraints and sickness she endured during long months on the road—she even dismisses malarial fever and a leg infection, joking with the doctor before he makes an incision. Rather, hardship lies in her inability to break through some kind of invisible—that is, non-physical—but nonetheless considerable barrier separating her from her lover, her home, her mother, her country. In short, from everything that is familiar.

And therefore, the inexorable conclusion the narrator comes to is that she will never make it back to comforts such as love and hope, but die alone 'at the end of the world', joining her lover in the next life as a bodiless creature—an angel rather than a flesh-and-blood, breathing human being.

This is a translation of the German original edited by Roger Perret for Lenos Verlag, Basel (1998), which was the first publication of a typescript entitled *Death in Persia* that Schwarzenbach wrote in August 1935 in the Lar Valley, Persia, and from January to March 1936 in Sils, Switzerland. Schwarzenbach's Persian trip in 1935 was her fourth visit to Asia—between 1932 and 1938, she would visit it six times in all. The original text sometimes alternates between the present and past tense within one section. This discrepancy, whether or not deliberate, shifts the narrative perspective from a memory being recounted to an event in progress, and could well be an amalgamation of various events that took place during previous trips. In 1935, she married a French diplomat, Claude Clarac, who is mentioned once by name in the chapter 'Ascent to the Happy Valley'. Place names that are anachronistic (for example, Stambul, Rages, Persia) have been retained. However, in the case of two alternatives (for example, Ghom/Qom), the translation is as phonetically similar to the original as possible.

Lucy Jones, 2013

Part One

PREFACE

This book will bring little joy to the reader. It will not even comfort him nor raise his spirits such as sad books very often can do according to a common belief that suffering has a moral strength if only endured in the proper way. I have even heard it said that death itself can be uplifting but I confess that I do not believe this—for how are we supposed to ignore its bitterness? It has a violence too, incomprehensible and inhumane, and our fear of it only diminishes if we come to expect it as the one admissible, final path to deliver us from our errant ways.

Yes, this book is about errant ways and its subject is despair. But if the author's sole aim is to rouse the sympathy of her readers, she is bound to fail in this case— for we can only hope for sympathy and understanding if our failures can be explained, our defeats are valiantly fought and our suffering is the inevitable consequence of rational events. Although we may be occasionally happy for no reason, it is unacceptable to be *unhappy* for no reason. And in difficult times like these, one is supposed to be effortlessly capable of selecting the enemy and the destiny that suits our strengths.

The heroine of this slim volume, however, is so unheroic that she cannot even name her enemy and so weak that she seems to give up the fight even before her ignominious defeat has been announced.

But this is not even the worst part—the reader will forgive the author much less for never making it clear why a person should drift as far as Persia only to surrender to nameless conflicts. There is talk more than once of deviations, escape routes and errant ways, and those living in a European country today know how few are able to bear such terrible tension—a tension that comes from the personal conflict between a need for calm and a need for decisiveness, or from financial hardship, whether minimal or overpowering, and the most fundamental, most pressing, political questions about our economic, social and cultural future in which no one gets off lightly. If young people still try to get off lightly—no matter how conscientiously they plan their escape—they bear the mark of Cain's betrayal on their foreheads.

This is more or less the position of the girl who wrote these notes. When I held the finished manuscript in my hands, it became clear that I should devise a story to precede it and therefore make it accessible to everyone. In doing so, the reader would be satisfied and the publisher would have a viable book. But this was precisely what I couldn't do for it would distort the book's real subject, and I would have been giving in to our spiritual and ethical needs in an unacceptable way. Because the hopelessness and desperate futility of every protest described here has nothing to do with escape (and therefore betrayal), as it might appear at the beginning. Our standards and explanations no longer count here. This is simply the story of a person who has reached the end of her strength.

There is a thin line between the unnatural and the preternatural, and Asia's desperate size is preternatural—not hostile, merely too vast. What significance does a single death have on this scale? And yet, nothing is more desperate than the words: 'Someone's dying!' No, making things up won't unburden me, or relieve you. The danger here is intangible, the fear nameless—this makes it all the more terrifying—and there are paths so terrible that there can be no return.

Why else die?

Death seems unnatural; it fills us with desperation. But Asians have incorporated it into their religions as 'the void'—the one true existence, or the one true strength. They await it without fear. Our lives, on the other hand, are inconceivable without this fear—it is the essence of our existence. Away from its sphere, torn from our familiar comforts—a face that breathes, a heart that beats, gentle landscapes—we must finally abandon ourselves to the high winds which tear our last hopes to shreds. Where should we turn? All round us is utter desolation—basalt-grey rock faces, leprous-yellow deserts, dead moon valleys, chalky brooks and silvery currents in which perished fish drift upstream. Where to? O helplessness, paralysed wings of the soul! Not even the passing of night and day pene-trates our consciousness although the day is bright and shadeless and the night is lit with cold stars.

One sometimes clings tightly to pain, to bitter home-sickness and bitter regret, but one forgets one's guilt; in vain, you might think back to the beginning (who led me this far?). If only you were allowed to accuse once more, turn to others once more, *love* once more! You plunge into the wide, ocean-like hallucination, you have faith and pray, and forget your dark fear when you gaze into the face of your beloved. But how should one fight it?

Oh! To awake once more without anxiety, not alone for once, not abandoned to fear! To feel the contented breathing of the world!

Oh! To live again!

IN TEHERAN

In Teheran, the heat was so intense that it seemed to brood in the walls like in round ovens. In the evenings, it would radiate out and fill the narrow alleys and the new, wide, shadeless streets; not a breath of air brought in a cool night breeze from outside. In the gardens of Shemiran, it was cooler. Once you left them, you were assaulted by a white, shimmering light; the mountain face of the Tochal rose up, pale grey and transparent from the heat that hung around it in swathes like a veil, obscuring too the dazzling sky and shrouding the plains in a white haze. A month ago, they had still seemed bright green, yellow and earthy brown—the grasslands, crops and ploughed fields. Now there was nothing but barren deserts and beyond Teheran, among the ruins of the ancient city of Rages, a surging dust cloud. There, along the road to Ghom, at night with their bells tinkling, camel caravans trailed . . .

Ghom is a holy city. If you drive along the road from Teheran to Isfahan, you can see its golden mosque from the road across a vast stretch of water but we take a detour round the city and cannot enter its bazaars and courtyards. There is another golden cupola in Shah Abdul Azim, the oasis town next to the ruins, and the most golden and most holy dome is in the city of Meshed, far in the northeast on the ancient road of Samarkand.

When, a few weeks ago, the Shah forbade the wearing of the kula Pahlavi—the hat named after him—and in its place recommended the wearing of European hats, but allowed women to remove the chador and even to go unveiled on the streets, there were reports here and there of protests, especially in the holy cities. The kula was undoubtedly a most nondescript, even ugly, cap that made its wearers look like troublemakers and brutes. Nevertheless, it was possible to turn the brim to the back, and so while performing prayer, in accordance with religious conventions, touch the ground with one's forehead without exposing one's head. This is simply impossible with a European fedora, boater or bowler, and this was the reason the mullahs believed their finest hour had come and prayed in secret groups and in mosque courtyards for all to hear.

One read in the newspapers about the jubilation with which people welcomed the civil reforms, and ministers and local governors gave dinners which female guests were required to attend without the chador. At the entrance, crowds jostled to see the spectacle of carriages from which ladies emerged in deep shame and bewilderment. During the meal, the servants removed the guests' kulas from the cloak rack, whereupon the male guests received a *farangi** hat prepared for their departure to avoid going home bareheaded. What exemplary, most Western, bureaucracy, not dissimilar to Peter the Great's removal of the Boyars' Asian beards! Those beards have survived in Persia; and in return, Iranian diplomats may wear a bicorn, which the West, stumbling drunk on progress, only introduced during the French Revolution along with human rights. One can see which has greater longevity. In Hungary, the Magyars—to be allowed a seat in Parliament and to prove their patriotism—had to grow long moustaches, dutifully waxing the ends into bold twirls. But where is the Shah supposed to find a model of how to introduce good old human rights?

Because of the kula Pahlavi, Teheran's bazaar remained closed for three days. Was the Holy Mosque in Meshed really under fire? It was rumoured that the soldiers had refused to shoot at their religious compatriots and holy sanctuaries and were therefore replaced by Israelis and Armenians. The number of fatalities is mentioned.

These were the hottest days of the Persian summer. Some gardens in Shemiran, surrounded by much-too-high walls and filled with much-too-lush greenery, became as airless and as hot as greenhouses. Mosquitos swarmed over stagnant ponds. I came down with malarial fever for the second time. At night, the air cooled outside a little but my fever rose. When I left the garden again for the first time, Teheran's surroundings were scorched.

* Derived from the Persian word for the Franks and was used in Persia to refer to Christians or Westerners in general.

The gardens lay like dark islands dotted among the dreary, leprous yellowness. In front of me, on the dirt road, walked a young officer, his shoes and gaiters quite white with dust. He was carrying a pouch, and his helmet in a box. I stopped and let him climb in. He smiled, sweat running down his sunburnt face. We drove past wasted fields, the air hanging above them, quivering in the heat, and through the small bazaar in Dezashib that seemed pitch black. Dotted in the gloom like bright spots were the traders' faces, the children and the women's white scarves. The square in Tajrish was large and empty except for the carriages and the thin, white horses that stood there, stupefied by the sun. I watched the officer walk away across the empty square through the shimmering light that glittered with dust. On the other side of the square, I saw a gendarme appear and make a sign with his hand that was clearly intended for me. But he surely didn't expect me to react: in the heat, everyone has enough work just dealing with himself . . .

Then, through the great gate into a garden. Darkness and shadows beat down on me in waves. It smells of coolness, of earth, of leaves—a driveway with tree roots that stick out on the path and jerk the car to one side if I take a corner too fast. In third gear up to the house! I leave the car in the shade, get out, walk over the white terrace, over to the double doors covered with fine mosquito netting. From the living room comes the sound of a piano playing. So Zadikka is still practising, I think, everything is as it was before. I breathe out after the long, nameless terror of the journey through the open countryside that is deformed and exhausted to death by the sun.

Zadikka is thirteen years old. She is one of the most beautiful creatures in the world. A hairband, like a sash across her forehead, holds back her dark hair, an old-fashioned, girlish hairstyle and a Nubian head—large, gentle, golden animal eyes set in a tender brown face. The base of her nose is wide; Zadikka always breathes through flared nostrils. She probes curiously, her voice is tender, caressing, childishly delighted. Like the heads of Akhen-aten's utterly graceful daughters, Zadikka has an open, petal-shaped mouth that is thrust slightly forward, a chin full of childish defiance, a very slender throat and a neck bent as though in pride and sorrow. She is childish for her age but also far more serious, attentive and reserved than is usual for her years. I am always watching her with fresh rapture.

Zadikka's eldest sister lies next to me under a large tree. We have been brought pillows and iced water in fogged glasses.

'I'm going away,' I say.

'To join your English friends?'

'Yes. At their site in the Lar Valley.'

'When?'

'Tomorrow.'

We remain silent for a while. Calls from the tennis court and the dry sound of balls being served reach our ears.

'What if you catch fever up there?'

I looked at her. She was resting on her elbows and her hair fell like a veil in front of her face. She was beautiful even if she looked nothing like her younger half-sister. I thought about how she had Circassian and Arab blood. I looked at her much-too-pale face, marked by weakness, and the feverish glaze of her eyes.

'And you?' I asked.

'I don't take my temperature any more,' she said, 'I always have fever. But with me, it's different. There's nothing that can be done.'

'The climate is bad for you,' I said.

She shrugged. 'For all of us,' she said, 'but there, you see, I can't go up to the Lar Valley! I wouldn't even survive the journey.'

'Shouldn't you try at least?'

She passed her hand lightly over my mouth. 'Stop that,' she said, 'you will feel wonderful up there.'

ASCENT TO THE HAPPY VALLEY

In Abala, the mules were waiting. It was eight o'clock in the morning, and the sun was sliding down over the pass towards us. Behind us lay the road that ran through Teheran's insipid desert plains, up through the sea of petrified hills, then up and down its yellow dunes to the summit of the pass before falling precipitously in terrifying bends down to the Rudahand Basin. A two-hour drive by car, yet everything was so far away now, everything was vanishing—before us, a new day!

Our route first led us through a valley that lay tightly tucked between the hills. The lushness of its river shores was cramped, spilling over, as though over the rim of a basket, to where it joined the slopes of the fields. There was a grove of nut trees and just beyond it, vines.

Then the pass began. I saw Claude in front of me, his pith helmet pushed back. The mules trod patiently over the gravel with their small hooves. The pass led high up to winds and fast-moving clouds. Then, across the far distant plain, the clouds dispersed and there was nothing to see except for the sea of sky and arid earth, airlessly embracing one another. We turned round. There, past a dip in the valley, lay that extraordinary mountain range made of nothing but sand—steep, vast, constantly trickling tiers, reminiscent of snowdrifts. Any moment, a tier might loosen and shift down into the valley, or the eerie trickling sound might intensify to form an avalanche. But the sand crowned a ridge of rocks, silver and unmoving against the blue sky.

We descended from the summit of the pass into the valley that was just a chasm between two mountains. Below there was nothing, a dead valley far removed from the world, far removed from plants and flowers, merely stone, and a ferocious heat that clung on as though it had a thousand tentacles. Grey vipers, grey lizards, lifeless and gently rolled up, life only showing in their eyes—black pinpricks—and tiny tongues.

Even in the dead, moon-like valleys, there had to be the occasional oasis. What we found was a circular pit, and in it a smooth surface of water, rippling slightly as though pulsing from the heartbeat of a bird through the thin trickle of water in the sand.

We drank, propped up on our arms. Our mules stood close by in a stupor, and on the stony hills sheep waited in a circle, their heads lowered and facing the centre, seeking their own shadows. They were waiting for the day to end.

As if sleepwalking, we began the ascent to the second pass. Not even the muleteers were singing now although their songs are surprisingly similar to the somnolent step of the mule caravans in the midday mountain wind.

We are high above the tree line. Above us, rocks soar high into the sky like cliffs into the ocean. And, suddenly, we see camels up there, like mythical creatures with out-stretched necks, striding strangely parallel to the narrow grass strips. They tug up grass in the same rhythm and raise their long necks at the same time too. They stop and are so big and threatening above that we are afraid they might just fall clumsily onto us. Instead, they trot upwards with swaying humps and swinging legs, and, right at the summit of the pass, our paths cross. Behind them, a mag-ical image, the cone of Mount Damavand, appears.

Then we continue towards the Damavand. The pass descends gently, leading us through a stone gorge that comes out into the wide valley basin. It takes an hour to cross—Mount Damavand does not appear smaller at the end. It is like the moon, a smooth cone, no matter what angle one looks at it from. In winter, it is white, a super-natural, cloud-like white. Then, in July, it is striped like a zebra. At the top, one can make out the soft fumaroles of sulphuric vapours rising from the ancient crater of Mount Bikni. This was the Assyrians' name for the mountain when they wrote that the new peoples of the 'Distant Medes' had settled all the way up to its foot-hills—but they knew nothing of its volcanic activity. For three thousand years, it has been extinct! Since time immemorial!

This wide basin is still not the Lar Valley. Many valleys, some named, others nameless, disgorge their foamy streams here, their sources lost in the blue mountain ranges. There are nomads' camps on the grass plains that we cross. Their black, goat-hair tents are the same as those in the Mesopotamian deserts or in the Kurdish mountains, in fertile Syria or in Palestine. I look down the path in front of me, and behind, I look across the ancient lands of the Middle East . . . at the end, this valley basin! Burnt, yellow! The black goats and Karakul sheep sweep across it, a fleecy mass, and the sound of their thousand scurrying hooves is like the rushing of the wind. A different rustling comes from a thousand locusts—we walk over their dry husks, their parchment-like wings and bodies, over living creatures—that is reminiscent of a raging firestorm.

My mule stumbles and falls. The posteen slips down over my neck, I leap to my feet. Had I fallen asleep? The muleteers curse. We continue . . .

Eight hours pass until we reach the far end of the basin where there is a narrow pass, a portal between two towering rocks. Beyond the bend in the path, down in the valley, the white tents stand.

THE WHITE TENTS OF OUR CAMP

The tents stand in a row on the grass slope close by the riverbank. These 'Swiss huts' are from India and are double-layered—a sunshade is stretched over the smaller inner shell that is lined with yellow material. This creates a small, shaded portico in front of each tent where one sits in the morning with books and writing materials while the river at one's feet glides swiftly and peacefully down the valley. Below, the steadfast, gleaming pyramid of Mount Damavand. On both sides of the valley is the grey rock face, a grey so lucid that it's almost silver, and above it, southwards, spotless and incredibly clear, the dark blue sky.

In the afternoon, the valley is white from the sun. At around five o'clock, when we fetch our fishing rods from behind the tent, the shadows grow longer. Up to now, the water has been silvery but soon it will turn black. Up to now, it has been a pleasure to get undressed and slip into the river, to let oneself be carried away by the strong current. You have to grip the round, smooth stones tightly. . . There is always wind on the riverbank; you dry off quickly, feeling the sun on your neck yet shivering at the same time . . .

On the other bank, opposite our camp, a chaikhana is set on a pile of shingle. Like our alpine huts, set on the highest sheep-grazing plains near the Julier Pass, it has been built under the shelter of the mountain slopes of round stones so that roof and slope merge into one. The Afjeh Pass ends here, an old bridle path that leads from the valley of Djard Rud over to the Lar and from there, round Mount Damavand, down to Mazandaran.

The name has a wonderful ring to it—Mazandaran, a tropical region on the Caspian Sea. The jungle rules there—rainforest, humidity, malaria. In Gilan, the western neighbouring province, the rice fields have been drained and the Chinese teach the malaria farmers the ancient art of tea cultivation. The small coastal towns are home to Russian caviar fish.

To the east, the steppes begin, grazing grounds for the Pendin and Teke Turkmen with their red-and-camel-coloured carpets, their rows of tents, their saddlebags. They breed horses, and seven-year-old youngsters ride them in autumn in the great steppe races. In the harbour of Krasnovodsk, the Russian railway begins, a lonesome stretch of track that runs through the steppe through Merv, Bukhara, Samarkand. Then we're close to the curly-haired Tajiks who live in their Soviet state up in the Pamir Mountains. Asia . . .

From our tents, we watch the bustle on the other side of the river. Mule caravans turn the bend accompanied by sounds of bells and muleteers' cries. Others come up into the valley and one sees them from afar. Donkeys arrive with their riders, sometimes camels. Caravans, nomads, soldiers. The soldiers, slant-eyed and darkly tanned, sit in their saddles with their legs stretched forwards, galloping on loose reins. They all stop at the chaikhana; many spend the night there.

By the river, where the grass grows abundantly, animals graze or roll about on the sandbanks. In the darkness, we see the red light of a fire across from us. It fills the chaikhana doorway and we see the men huddled round the samovar . . .

MEMORIES OF MOSCOW

Beginning of August. This time last year, I was in Russia. It was hot, the streets of Moscow were scorching, there were always white clouds in the sky and planes crisscrossed over the airfield, lurched, then caught themselves like swallows before the outbreak of a storm. Parachuting was all the rage among the young. From five or six thousand feet, the jumpers would leap into the vertiginous void, letting themselves fall, and sing so as not to be killed by the air pressure. Fragments of their heroic songs reached our ears. Then, already very low, already level with the silver tips of the radio towers, they ripped open their parachutes and sailed slowly to the ground. How long did it take? Minutes? We saw them falling, awfully slowly, then floating. All in the space of a split second. A seventeen-year-old worker jumped from three thousand metres and was killed. She was found afterwards, her hands clamped to her shoulder straps instead of the ripcord that would have released the canopy. Would they claim she was 'a heroine of the people'?

Ambition spurred on the young who, in white aprons or oily metro-worker overalls, filled the streets. Until late at night. On Youth Day, it took ten hours for them to cross Red Square. And every day they crowded in front of Congress Hall and in the corridors of old noble houses to see the poets—first Gorki, then all the young ones. And books were demanded of them, books on Russia, on sailors, on aeroplanes, on scientists, on metro-workers, on kolkhoz labourers, on women and schoolchildren and parachute heroes. It could make one fear for art . . .

'What do you want in Persia?' Malraux asked me. He knew the ruins of the city of Rages. He also shared a passion for archaeology. He had thought hard about human passions and seen through them, and he tended to attach little value to them except for what was left of them in the end—suffering. 'Just for the sake of the name? Just for the sake of being *far away*?'

And I thought of Persia's terrible sadness . . .

I often spent time with Eva back then. Her husband was a member of the Party, and spoke seriously and passionately about the need, in modern times and especially present times, to fight for a community that would be the society of the future.

He called himself 'comrade'—*tovarish*—and yet was so alone in the Party, set apart in the way that people with extraordinary talents always are, longing for approval. He had been a Jesuit pupil, had rejected the 'credo quia absurdum' in bitter disappointment, had forsaken higher spiritual fulfilment and refused the compromise that

accepted the world's failings by denying they existed—
the compromise that kept the masses in suffering submission, deferred their right to happiness to the hereafter,
and even abused the revolutionary instinct in the young
(an eternal safeguard against progress in thinking) through
militant discipline and the idealization of sacrifice,
knowing how to put it to the service of present political
circumstances. He had rejected all this in the face of
the violence and sheer misery and plight, the growing
backlash and suffering of his fellow human beings.

'Have you read Spengler's *Entscheidung*?'* he asked.
'So brilliant, so much foresight . . . but as a "courageous
pessimist", why does he insist on taking sides with the
dying world? Why does he hate everything new and inno-
vative or still in the throes of birth and the problems of
youth? Workers, the continent of Asia, and its people
awakening to a political conscience? Why should monar-
chies—no matter whether they have constitutions, their
armies can't stop the tragic upheavals of history—have
preference over everything modern? He's inflexible, vain
and servile towards the rulers of the world. But we are a
generation determined to fight and die, and the least we
want is to be on the side of the future.'

He worked day and night. Exhausted, skeletal, consumed by an inner inferno, he resembled a militant monk,
sometimes a scholar. He dressed in the bourgeois style,
casually wearing dark-blue suits with a tie. His wife was

* Oswald Spengler, *Jahre der Entscheidung* (Munich: C. H. Beck
Verlag,1933). Translated into English by Charles France Atkin-
son as *The Hour of Decision* (New York: Alfred A. Knopf, 1934).

petite, blonde, quiet, and consumed by homesickness. She had grown up on a farm in Holstein and that was where she should have stayed with her younger brothers, busy preserving fruit, baking, tending the chicken coop and a large flower bed. Her husband was now due to leave for a six-month trip to Siberia. She was afraid.

'What do you expect?' he asked—the three of us were having a late meal—'The Revolution isn't child's play and it's not going to take place at a writer's congress.'

'Can't you take me with you?'

'Impossible! You'd just be in my way.'

'Then perhaps—Switzerland?' she asked shyly.

'Switzerland!' he repeated in an angry tone, 'To Ascona, to friends—why not just go to Germany? Are you *serious?*'

She wept.

'Can't you explain to Eva?' he asked, turning to me. 'I want her to stay in Moscow and join a weaving mill. Please tell her why. Because in front of my comrades I can't afford to have a wife who likes going to Ascona on pleasure trips. My wife has to do her part.'

'She's homesick,' I answered.

'And you?' he retorted harshly, 'aren't you homesick? Why have *you* chosen an uncomfortable life?'

He left for some evening meeting. Eva and I stayed at the table. She's thinking of Holstein, I imagined, a meadow in Holstein with patchwork cows and blackberry bushes. And my thoughts turned to my lakeside home . . .

Eva stopped crying.

One day I found myself alone on a small Russian steamship on the Caspian Sea and I came ashore the next evening in Pahlavi. It was raining. A sea eagle was crouching on the rainswept sand, looking out to sea. It was September, the summer was over, and Russia was over too. I'd seen the vineyards, the green hills of Georgia vanishing, and, in the semi-desert between Tiflis and Baku, Asia returned, a caravan trail far into the distance with the first camels . . .

The Georgian military road was nothing but a memory—the gorges with cool, gurgling water and the high ranges of rocks, and beyond, suddenly appearing in the blue sky, the peak of the Kazbek. The summer evening in the villages . . .

A friend picked me up in Pahlavi. We drove along the beach, so close to the water's edge that, at times, a wave rolled under the wheels and leapt up high like a flag. The damp sand was heavy, like snow. It grew dark. Behind the dunes in the mist and twilight lay the jungle of Rasht. Through the mist, fires glowed in open huts where Gilan farmers sat beneath low straw roofs. One saw their ghostly-pale, malaria-stricken faces next to the reddish lamps. The wind rustled through the trees that had grown wizened in the summer and were now shedding their leaves. The bazaar alleyways in the villages were illuminated—in every shop a lamp was lit, and the bakers stood in the light of their round ovens and threw the lightly-browned, flat loaves onto a cloth to dry. There were melons and aubergines to buy, dark green and violet, and hundreds of vegetables and spices. There was vodka and arak in white bottles. The traders crouched low, unmoving, behind their baskets.

We spent the night in Rasht. The next day it wouldn't stop raining. We drove through the Sefid Rud Valley and up the great Qazvin Pass. Beyond lay the plain and, in an oasis, the city of Qazvin. Behind its colourful city gate, the plain spread out all the way down to Teheran.

AT THE END OF THE WORLD . . .

We sometimes call this valley 'the end of the world' because it is high above the earth's plains and there is nothing higher except the ethereal—the otherworldliness that touches the heavens—or the smooth peak of the giant mountain. It obstructs the exit from the valley but, when one advances on its snow-streaked bulk, it is as distant as the moon, a wonderful sight.

I say 'exit from the valley', so there must be a path leading down somewhere? And its water must flow out somewhere? The shepherds indicate with their hands—to the right, around Mount Damavand's base. (How big can its base be? Down inside where the water flows, does a fire still burn and molten rock boil?)

Yes, the valley leads down to Mazandaran. First, through green alpine meadows. Then through woods that soon turn into a rainforest full of bears, wolves, panthers and wildcats. Then the tropical jungle, then the dunes. Then, at last, the Caspian Sea, grey between the windswept plains. The villages are magical—animal skulls bleach on their slopes, a spell surrounds them, a perfect stillness of the wind. But in the shelter of the dunes that cut them off from the sea, like an embankment, one senses a restless rustling, and, above it, the cries of birds trailing eastwards into the steppe . . .

The Lar Valley disappears where the river thins, dividing into several arms among the black cliffs. The arms course out again onto a plain, a wide basin where nomads pitch their tents. In the evening, the water is still, as specular as silver, like veins in the shadowy grass. Behind it tower the rocks. Oh, to climb them! To look out over the roof of Asia, at its bordering mountains and abysses! Down the pass of the Old Lady, to the azure of the Persian Gulf, to Bandar-e Bushehr and Bandar-e Abbas, its narrow harbour towns. The European consulates are falling apart there, and a left-behind English civil servant goes every evening at about seven o'clock to the hotel bar on the harbour, sits among the smugglers and harbour police in white evening dress, and sips his martini. It is hot down there. The ships that dock have purple sails. Sometimes, one sees a fire on the dark horizon and imagines that a ship has been set ablaze. But it is just the rising moon. Sometimes, sandstorms come up and strike the coast that lies withering in the sun—four hours earlier, the storm raced through India, was reported in Karachi and flew over the deserts of Balochistan. Then, like snow, the sand lies in the houses of Bushehr. Outside, the Bakhtiari people wait in their mountains, and the Arabs, their keffiyehs wrapped round their mouths and ears. Sand devils race through the night; entire hills rise up and storm off. Animals lie asphyxiated in their path, gazelles, their beautiful eyes destroyed . . .

'And he surveyed the beauty of the world'—far out, on the last street that leads to the sea, lies the island of Hormuz, once a treasure protected by the Portuguese. The ruins are stone blocks covered with dense undergrowth, reminiscent of the fortresses and churches in Mexico. But far from this, on the high plain, circling the mountains like great ships, the columns of Persepolis still stand. The royal terrace rises to half the height of the mountain and is an expanse of ruins from a sublime past. Sometimes, snow lies there. High up above the graves of the Achaemenids flocks of ibex and mouflon wander, their compact bodies with strong horns twisting backwards like curls. At night, guards watch over the tombs. The flames from their torches bring the reliefs to life and they seem to slide down the high walls, the ghostly features of hunters, shepherds, tribute-bearers and kings.

On the white, moon-like plain below, the huge shepherd dogs sleep with the fleecy herds. On the road to Shiraz stands a modest adobe chaikhana; trucks fill the courtyard and piles of petrol cans. Taxi-drivers sit here, workers, and an opium-smoker. They gaze up at the terraces where their kings' palaces once stood. Alexander the Great, after a banquet, drunk and full of love for the treasures of Darius' library, yet equally full of hate for them, set the palaces on fire. It was like an apocalypse when the roof, supported by mighty columns and animal's bodies, collapsed. Smoke and fire was lifted by the mountain wind and, in a murky cloud, swept off across the terrace and out onto the plain. This spectacle of destruction pleased the youthful king and his soldiers sped with immoral greed, like phantoms, through the flames, looting and stealing before they were struck by falling timber . . .

The people in this country are so terribly solitary! One would have to wear seven-league boots to get from one village to the next, and what separates each place is desert, rock—different kinds of wilderness. In the thirteenth century, the Mongols came from the Asian plains and overran the Persian towns. Arabic writers tell of how a million were slaughtered in the prosperous town of Rages alone. In the mountain village of Damavand, farmers fled to the mosques but in vain—the Mongolian riders chased them through the alleys and murdered them all. They even sought out Alamut, the fortress of the 'Old Man of the Mountain' hidden in a rock in the Elburz Mountains from where the Ismaelites sent down their hashish-eating youths as assassins, across the desert, to the Crusader's town of Antioch and then to Egypt. The fortress of Alamut was legendary—one could only reach it with a rope ladder—but the Mongols found it and razed it to the ground.

Back then, the people of the flatlands fled to the hills—as they did too when Persia was haunted by the sword of Islam. The most distant villages thus have Persian names and their inhabitants have not intermingled with Arabs or Mongols. High mountain ranges cut them off from one another. On the plain are empty half-deserts, undulating moon landscapes which, in the drifting light, are set in motion like the sea. And endless, endlessly straight, the road runs through it. On the crest of a hill, far below to the south, lies the town of Yazd, encircling the ridge, house to house like a fortress and casting the shadow of its fantastic silhouette down upon the plain. But the houses are decrepit—the masonry crumbling between wooden beams and the wind whistling through empty windows. Running round the rocks and the city is a wide, bright green strip of grass where sheep graze—the only touch of charm.

These are the people of the villages, the plains, the dunes and swamps of Mazandaran, the harbour towns on the Gulf. These are the nomads of the Bakhtiari Mountains, the shepherds, the horse-breeders in the Turkmen Steppe, the caviar fishermen. These are the farmers and traders in the bazaar and the craftsmen: bakers and coppersmiths, lacquer painters and carpet washers. These are the caravan-herders, the truck-drivers. The workers and the soldiers. The beggars. I once asked in Moscow why no one promoted Communist propaganda in neighbouring Iran. The Persians were, after all, the poorest of all people.

'It's impossible,' came the reply, 'There is no solidarity, no common consciousness. They are so alone that they are not even aware of their poverty and misery. And they don't know that there might be a better life, a happier one. They believe that God has punished each individual with unhappiness.'

But much lonelier than Yazd and the isolated mountain villages and the tents of the steppe nomads, much lonelier still, is the Lar Valley; it is past humanity as it is past the tree line. And the nomads and muleteers who trail through the valley in summer leave it again after a few months. And the snow covers it over.

. . . AND A PERSON
AT THE END OF HER STRENGTH

> Do you recall our unruffled hours, when we and
> we alone were rapt to one another? How tri-
> umphant! The two of us so free and proud and
> alert, blossoming, beaming in soul and heart,
> and eye and face, each of us alongside the other
> in such heavenly bliss!
>
> *Hölderlin**

What happens, though, when a person has reached the
end of her strength? (Not through sickness, or pain, or
misfortune, but worse.) She sits one morning in front of

---

* David Farrel Krell, *The Recalcitrant Art*: *Diotima's Letters to
Hölderlin and Related Missives* (Douglas F. Kenney and Sabine
Menner-Bettscheid trans) (Albany, NY: State University of New
York Press, 2000), p. 121.

her tent and looks out over the river. On the other side, mules stand in the long grasses of the riverbank. A light wind bends them, like corn in a field, and carries smoke up to the pass from the chaikhana door. The Shah's horse-tenders arrive from the meadow on their panting, white or piebald steeds, driving them on with cries as they gallop over the shingle shore. The sun is strong, white and noonday-ish. It's as though the wind is chasing the riders along like clouds or dust from volleys of gunfire. Your eyes tire of gazing across—grey rocks, blue basalt, hopelessly painful. If you stare long enough at the black, fast-moving, patchy water, you grow dizzy and feels something akin to dread.

Stand up, you think, stretch your aching back. In the afternoon hours, lying half-stretched in the warm twilight of the tent on the camp bed, you realize that there is no rest. And then the hopeless terror of night! It will pass, and another day will begin with a grey, yellow, golden dawn and the wonderful metamorphosis of the river will begin—a moon stream at night, black yet as specular as a mirror, branching out, shallow, making hills recede and rocks retreat. A long, endlessly stretching moon-river, in which fish glide, sleeping or perished, bellies upended.

In the day, a rapid mountain stream, slipping silvery over stones in sunspots. A different day!

But what should you do? Was yesterday not full of a thousand possibilities? Meadow walks and drifting down-river, climbing on rocks, raw burning stone under your grazed hands; a wide vista across the valley with its shep-herds and herds and nomads' tents, its hundred and fifty horses, its white sandbanks. Light, suspended clouds or smoke around the Damavand, sleep and dreamy warmth, and, in the evening, wading along the river and casting the line. That was the life!

What has changed since then? You raise your hand slowly and clench your fist. Impossible to clench a fist. You feel weak, insipid, a dreadful, debilitating listlessness, worse than malarial fever in your back, in your knees, in your neck. Your hands grow damp, speaking requires too much effort. Get up and walk! With fast, hammering heart, you walk along the riverbank, more briskly so as not to succumb to the temptation to throw yourself to the ground, weeping with exhaustion and despair. Ah, but you will not weep. It is far, far worse. You are alone.

The wind and mountains are not even hostile— merely too vast. One is forsaken among them, and everything is meaningless, all exertion is carried off by the wind . . . If only you could flee, you think, and it is only self-preservation that forces you to go on. You begin to stammer the names of the people you think you love. Dreadful, how they too are carried away, their faces ripped to shreds, their eyes staring unseeingly, their bodies far, far away, unreachable, forsaken . . . No, you think, suddenly in desperation—this can't go on, not for a quarter of an hour longer, you have to find something, find a remedy, and you grip your belt, your hips, with your fists, clench everything, shake yourself. Suddenly, you realize that all the time your jaw was clenched. You are drenched in sweat, short of breath, the fear in your heart again almost like nausea, and you are at the end, the end—

You kneel, half-stretched in the wind. It will continue like this, you think, always. Mother, you think (how the name makes you weep!)—I did something wrong, right at the beginning. But it wasn't me, it was life itself. All the paths—those I took, those I avoided—have ended here in this 'Happy Valley' from which there is no exit and so it is a place like death. Soft evening shadows fill it, softly gliding down the last mountains to cover the slopes and the sleeping herds that cling to them like down. And softly, in the twilight of the night, peaks and ridges emerge, one after the other. Scenes from the end of the world.

You stand up, slightly comforted. Timidly, you think of the possibilities that lie, as though in fog, in the far distance beyond this country. Of milder surroundings, with green hills, blue lakes, white sails, cheerfulness, even of towns, of views from windows onto bustling streets, of a ship's horn in a harbour, of dark wine bars in a small town, of a street that winds over the hills and along the lake towards home. Timidly and passionately, you search for a face suffused with warmth that will help you back to faithful, breath-inhaling life. Ah, one day, you will be helped after all . . .

And on the way back, the valley wind now behind you, you avoid going along the river; you are afraid that, on the banks, where the water is deep and dark and flows slowly, you might slide down and press your face into the coolness for as long as it takes for every restless and painful sensation to be over. You follow the mule path and keep your eyes on the tents.

THE ANGEL
(for Cathalene Crane)

That same night an angel entered my tent. From my camp bed I saw him draw back the flap and enter without stooping, even though for me, for my mortal height, the entrance was too low. He stood in the shadows yet was visible.

'I have returned,' I said.

He stood there but I don't know if he looked at me. His gaze must have been directed outside towards the night-time mountain valley and he shimmered like the gentle snowy heights of the Damavand.

'It was difficult enough,' I said, hesitatingly.

'Yes,' said the angel, 'it was difficult because I was fighting with you.'

Then I remembered that I had fought with the angel for my life, believing I was forsaken.

'I had an almost irrepressible urge,' I said, 'to slide down the riverbank and push my face into the cool, dark, water of death. Yes, I wanted to die.' I saw him nod. 'That is just the latest temptation,' I continued, 'not the worst. I left the tents when I couldn't bear it any longer—'

'—when you *thought* you could bear it no longer,' he corrected me.

'—and walked through the long grass that grows on the riverbank, and through the low grass full of locusts, and across the fields. The wind blew in my face and I wanted to turn back and throw myself to the ground and have no more to do with it all. I almost did . . .'

'But you carried on.'

'But I carried on, and the wind blew in my face. I crossed ridges, avoiding the grazing camels, avoiding the sheepdogs.'

'You could not avoid me,' said the angel.

'Then I crossed the valley basin. Did you see how I clenched my teeth together and thrust my fists in my belt but didn't cry out or weep?'

He did not answer. I could only hear the wind pulling at the ropes and the sides of the tent.

'And then?' asked the angel.

'Then I came to a hill that at first seemed impossibly far away. It was a hill of ruins from a long time ago. I'd already reached the shadows of the plain. The sun was setting on the distant mountains, ablaze, but I shuddered.'

'What did you do on the hill?'

'I bent down, for there were shards and pieces of clay tiles. I picked them up and carried them to the middle of the hill where, long ago, a thief or someone with a thirst for knowledge had dug up a funnel. That's where I saw the foundation of an old fortress—'

'Did you not see me?' asked the angel gently.

I said nothing. My eyes shut and my limbs paralysed, I lay on the narrow bed and listened. I could hear my heart beating unnaturally fast, and suddenly the pain in my back, the exhaustion in my slightly bent legs, the damp slackness in my hands. Sleep was far away and the wind, trapped in the valley basin, was tearing at the sides of my tent.

'Dear angel,' I said, 'dear angel, help me!' And, seized with fear, I opened my eyes.

He was standing in the middle of the tent; the delicate, matt light of the Damavand cloud was swathing his silhouette.

'On the hill,' he said, 'I began to fight for you. I saw your pain. I saw you torturing yourself, against every better instinct, hoping for a miracle. What was the matter?'

This dreadful question left me speechless. And I was overcome by the familiar, hopeless desperation.

'I don't know,' I answered.

But he did not insist that I pray or trust him as people, priests and doctors tend to do.

He came nearer. 'I saw you,' he said, 'I saw you climb the mountain ridges and walk through the valley basin and of course I noticed that you were at the end of your strength. If only you had found a foothold—a foothold to justify yourself to others, a foothold for your weary feet. But I saw too that you had no strength left to stand all this and so you wished to die.'

He leant towards me. 'For you are weak,' he said, 'the weakest of them all, but you are sincere. And therefore I decided to fight for you, to lift your fear of death.'

'I was not afraid,' I said softly.

'Your fear,' said the angel, 'was so great that you wanted to hide your face, in the long and the short grass, and in the deep water of death.'

At this, I fell silent.

'Do not believe that I can relieve you of anything,' said the angel.

I sighed deeply.

'What are you thinking?' asked the angel, who was so near now that I could have easily touched him.

'I'm thinking,' I said, 'that if only you would let me touch you then it would be easier for me. If only I were allowed to reach out my hand!'

'You cannot move,' said the angel pleasantly, 'you are utterly helpless and exposed to the angels of this land, who are terrible creatures. Do not have false hope. Even my decision to fight for you means nothing so far. Do you remember how, on the hill, you stood up, your hands full of shards? You thought you were fighting the wind, the evening chill. But you pulled yourself up on me and then I released you. And so you went back through the valley basin, encouraged, if not comforted, to the tents.'

'I was careful not to go near the river.'

'So you valued your life again?'

'No,' I said. 'The wind tore to shreds the faces of those I love.'

'I did not come here to relieve you of anything,' said the angel. 'Not for *that*. I just wanted to see how you are. I wanted to see if you could now bear the bleakness and solitude of my country.'

'Your country?' I asked, doubtingly.

'Do not expect too much from me,' he said harshly. 'We angels are also bound. There are thousands of angels in this country that you may meet and grasp for the sake of your salvation. But you have no guardian angel like they told you back home. There is nothing that can remedy your solitude. Out here, you have to be content to be one in a thousand . . .'

'I'm not discontent,' I dared to argue, 'I'm just so alone and don't know what I should hold on to or prop myself up with. You helped me again today, which was exhausting enough, but I don't meet an angel every day. Still, every day the sun rises and sets like burning hellfire, full of empty hours that amuse themselves but not me.'

'Express yourself more clearly,' said the angel severely.

I tried to clench my fists, which lay slack at my sides. It was dreadful how this feeling of vulnerability seeped through my limp body to my heart.

'I am afraid,' I said and looked at the angel. Or rather, I tried to look at him. I hoped his gaze would rescue me again and relieve the spasm round my heart, or fill my hands with strength.

But he was standing in the shadows. And I realized with a sudden desperation that he was not a human being I could cling to or feel a common desperation with, even if only to sob together.

Exhausted to death, I said, 'I can't go on any more.'

He simply said, 'You are sincere to the point of obstinacy. That does not help much when you have to deal with forces which are stronger than you—than all of you.'

And he left.

I didn't want to watch him pull back the flap and leave without stooping.

Outside, I thought, it's *his* country that welcomes him, *his* night, *his* wind. I couldn't help hearing the wind tearing at the ropes and sides of the tent. I saw the angel leaving, the gentle light of the Damavand like a cloak over his shoulders. Then he walked through the long grass on the riverbank and past the hundred and fifty horses that stood sleeping. Then he went through the river, without getting wet, past the crimson fire of the chaikhana, below the grey ledges where ibex spent the night. I lost sight of him, wondering why it hadn't been possible to keep him here, even though he'd fought for me on the hill of shards . . .

But I hadn't even been able to reach out my hand. And then, no one was there.

MEMORIES: PERSEPOLIS

We drove along the main road through the spacious, sweltering, dreamscape of the Persian plains. The road was the same one along which, after the apocalyptic inferno of Persepolis many centuries ago, Alexander the Great's soldiers had marched northwards to capture the fleeing King Darius III. The king was on the run. He had been courageous but after losing the Battle of Gaugamela, he was powerless to do more and so he fled without stopping across the Kurdish Mountains, through its lands of Media and Bactria, until his satrap Bessos murdered him.

The Persian plain has not changed since and will probably never change. On the fringes, mountain ranges lie dormant like stranded ships; one believes they come nearer but on reaching them, another plain begins which is in fact the same one and so you never reach the edge.

I remarked on this to Barbara, who was sitting beside me in the car.

'We'll never arrive in Persepolis,' I said, 'We won't survive the journey.'

'Four hundred kilometres?' she said, 'Surely you've survived that before?'

'Exactly!' I said, 'The first time, you risk everything because you are innocent. But after that, you should never be tempted again!'

'In that case,' replied Barbara, 'it was *me* who tempted *you*. I persuaded you to come on this trip. Don't tell me you regret it!'

'I would have tried again no matter what.'

'No matter what?'

'You have to be twice as sure about the things that you love in this country.'

'Are you struggling because it all seems like a dream?'

'Yes,' I said, 'It's frightening. I'm afraid of how fleeting things are.'

Yet even the name Persepolis was immortal and impenetrable, the view of the ruins unforgettable.

'This country makes cowards of people,' said Barbara.

We had to drive for many hours until it cooled down, and then many more hours in the dark. Yazd reared up over the ridge and glared so brightly in the sun that at first we thought it was a mirage. But this beggar's town, where leprous children clambered out of their dens and crumbling windows to surround our car, was certainly real.

Rashid drove for ten hours without growing tired. He always managed to light his cigarettes with a single match. This made Barbara envious. I slept, my head resting on my folded arms.

We stopped once in a city to buy gasoline. We were told that we still had to drive six or sixty parasang. Even if it was sixty parasang, Rashid said, we had enough gasoline. A parasang is an ancient unit of measurement from the city of Pasargadae; it took Persian troops an hour to travel one.

I began to weep.

'Do you want to spend the night here?' asked Barbara. I stopped weeping and we continued driving.

I don't know if we then drove through the forest of the farr people,* where the road dropped in steep bends, or how we finally reached the plain where Persepolis lay, still far off in the distance.

We saw its columns in the moonlight, turned off the road and I recognized everything and embraced Barbara with joy.

When we went out onto the terrace a short time later, Rashid was asleep, lying on a camp bed next to our car.

It was a large, moonlit, Persepolis night. From the terrace that hung as though suspended by ropes over the plain, the furthest edge of the footless mountains emerged from the darkness, a silvery strip outlining their dark bulks. Celestial light infused everything—mountains, plains and the reliefs on the royal staircase. The world lay

---

* In contemporary Persian and Tajiki languages, used to distinguish the peoples who lived in Central Asia and Iran in medieval and ancient times.

in a light slumber; a breath of wind could have awoken it. Past the rocks, where the Achaemenids lay buried deep in their tombs, the clouds soared and reached palely towards the Milky Way in almost carefree ascent. They grew more numerous, spreading in droves across the lofty space, covering the moon in gentle contrast to the sky's steely blueness. The earth lay in shadow.

'Everything's the same,' I said, and my friend Richard repeated my words. 'Exactly the same. Do you remember?'

I remembered. The same evenings, the same drunkenness, the same serenity, the same grief, the same excitement at the same ethereal, indifferent peace of this place. But back then I'd felt protected because a man had been here whose cleverness and love of the ancient past had saved Persepolis from oblivion and made it into a site of research and industry. But the professor had left. The books in his library lay packed in boxes in Bushehr, waiting to be sent to England or America or wherever his nomadic life took him next. The high windows of his study used to be lit all night; now, they lay in darkness among the stone pillars of Darius' harem that had been raised up again and crowned with beams and bulls' heads made of wood.

'The professor didn't always make it easy for us,' Richard said. 'He was so reclusive that we hardly dared to talk to him. And he didn't even take much notice of our work—he never praised us. But now I wish he'd come back . . .'

So, something had changed then—something significant.

A great scholar had been driven from his homeland for being a Jew, and now he'd been forced to leave his adopted home too, the royal castle of the ancient Aryans . . . 'Especially in times like these,' a German diplomat of distinction had once said to me, 'the professor, as a non-Aryan, should have been particularly tactful.'

'Yes,' said Richard, thoughtfully, 'that's the disgraceful logic of these people.'

The professor's successors were young Americans, willing excavators, boy scouts. None of them could decipher so much as one cuneiform inscription.

'Even if they could,' said Richard, 'even if they send over good people, it won't be the same.'

Mutual friends in Teheran had given me the task of reconciling Richard to the new situation, of persuading him to stay.

'And you?' I asked, 'Will you stick it out? You're important here, aren't you?'

'Stick it out?' he asked. He was standing far from me in the shadow of a door. Above him, a bearded genius spread his solitary wings.

'You love this place,' I said.

He nodded. 'Four years,' he said, 'it's been four years since I visited Germany . . . The Americans hate Germany. They hate it in a way that only uneducated people are able to hate. They don't know that the swastika is not Germany, and they forget that the professor was a German too.'

'Can't you explain it to them?'

'Me?' he asked.

'You know so many things.'

'I don't know a thing. For years, I've been homesick for a Germany that no longer exists. And what it's become can't be excused. It just can't!'

'No.'

'And that's why I have to listen to their hatred and contempt and jokes all day long. Apart from everything, my mother's Jewish.'

I said nothing, deeply concerned.

Richard didn't seem to expect an answer. He stood for a while, not saying anything, his head raised. I looked at his hard, boyish face, his angular jaw thrust forward, his low, square forehead in a frown, his thick eyebrows knitted together. Then he slowly came over to me.

'You of all people,' he said, 'shouldn't talk of sticking things out. You know it doesn't happen here and there's no sense in it.'

'So you want to leave?'

He nodded.

'And what will happen to you? Do you want to go to Germany?'

'To visit my mother, but that's all.'

'And after that?'

He shrugged.

'Come,' he said, 'the others are waiting.'

We went down the steps and back to the expedition house.

'You have to give yourself some time,' I said. 'You've been patient for four years out here. So it's hard to judge what's going on at home.'

'Yes, I'll give myself time.'

I would have liked to say something comforting. Patience is no comfort for a twenty-five-year-old, and only impatience was able to separate him from Persepolis. But that meant saving him from this country too.

'You understand why I can't stay here,' said Richard when we were standing in front of his room.

'Yes,' I said, 'you mustn't stay much longer.'

In Richard's room sat Barbara and young Heynes, a fellow American. Heynes was already slightly drunk. They were having an intense debate about Roosevelt and the National Recovery Administration. Heynes was barely able to counter Barbara's wonderfully concise arguments. He was trying to play the sceptic but she was protesting in her deep, strident voice.

'Where will it lead us if even young people like you aren't interested in the future? The future, our American future, should be something close to all our hearts. Roosevelt has reached out a hand—all we have to do is *take* it! In the office, we worked all day and half the night. And at lunchtime we sat together and talked. Because we have to *talk* about things, you must see that—we have to be *intelligent*!'

'What's the point?' asked Heynes, leaning his head on the back of the chair, 'What's the use of knowing that you can't solve the Black issue? That America is a pile of problems our best men fail to solve? What's the use of it all?'

'If only you knew,' wailed Barbara with feeling, 'how terrible things would be if the NRA collapsed! How much that would affect us all!'

Heynes laughed sleepily. 'There you go!'

'And you,' she asked, 'you take care of Achaemenian palaces in Persia ('in this rotten country,' she said) and you think can stay away from it all? Do you really believe *it's got nothing to do with you at all*?'

He fell silent. Richard, standing beside me in the doorway, butted in. 'What do you know about Persia?' he said. 'And anyway, Heynes is an architect like me, so it's enlightening *and* interesting to take care of Achaemenian palaces!'

Barbara turned her beautiful head in a quick movement. 'There you are.' she said. 'It seems we don't have anything left to drink!' She raised her empty glass to us.

We tossed a silver toman coin to see who'd be the one to drive to the tavern in the sugar factory for alcohol. The lot fell to Richard. I drove with him.

The sugar factory lay below on the plain. We saw its lights as we turned off the terrace into the road from Shiraz. The wind swept the dust cloud from the car into our path, and the headlights shone through it as if through a wall of fog. Richard sat in the driving seat. At least he wasn't drunk.

'It's nice of you to come with me,' he said.

'In the past,' I said, 'we used to drive the whole night together. Through the river to Naqsh-e Rustam and all the way to Isfahan.'

'In the past,' said Richard. He kept his gaze fixed ahead, as stubborn as all solitary people are.

'It wasn't that long ago,' I said hesitatingly, since it was only last year but it seemed like an eternity.

'We're nearly there,' he said, still looking ahead. In front of us lay the wall of fog, lit by yellow light.

'I wish we could drive to Naqsh-e Rustam like before,' I said.

'The river is in between.'

'Or to the end of the world.'

'But we're already at the end of the world.'

We pulled into the forecourt of the sugar factory. We had to get out, go over to the barracks, open a door, take the sudden blast of thick fumes in the yellow gloom and the enquiring looks of many Persian faces. The man behind the bar was Russian.

'Do you have any vodka?' asked Richard. We bought two bottles. While we waited, we had time to look about. Gathered here was what might be called the scum of Persia. There were nomads among them, rejected by their tribes, tempted by the lure of another life; driven-out Lurs were among them too, and homeless men from small towns and cities. They sat there, their strangely similar gaunt, yellow faces, their oddly shapeless bodies in squalid clothes imported from America and sold in bulk in Bushehr because the Persian national dress had been forbidden by the forward-thinking government. They were smoking opium. They sat apart from the regular drinkers in a corner close to a clay oven where an enormous samovar stood. If a European asked what was going on back there, he was told: 'Those men are ill.' But most of the time they were hungry and numbed by the sweet-smelling smoke, squatting on their carpets like animals, growling at strangers.

We paid the Russian for our bottles of vodka. Outside, the moonlight shone white on the sand. We spun the car round and drove back. I sat beside Richard, an arm round his shoulder. We were friends, like in times past, times that would not return. And again there was the long road, as straight as an arrow through the shimmering wall of fog, and the sudden apparition of the solitary columns of Persepolis on the terrace that seemed surreally suspended high above the plain.

We entered Richard's room and found Heynes there alone. Barbara had gone to bed, he said. We sat down, and Richard opened a bottle. Heynes, talkative and drunk, explained the new plans for the fortress construction. How they would no longer be drawn up at a variant of thirty degrees from the North, as the old professor had wished according to the ancient grounds of Persepolis, but drawn in ten-by-ten metre squares facing North and South, as was ordinarily done.

'And what'll happen to my plans?' asked Richard.

'Your plans? But they're all out of date,' said Heynes pleasantly.

'And the professor's publications?'

'They haven't been published yet!'

'He based them on the thirty degrees.'

'All out of date!'

'So,' said Richard, '*that's* your little game!'

'We respect your professor,' said Heynes, in a placating tone, 'but surely you understand that we can't work with outdated plans!'

'Of course not,' said Richard, '*you*, of course, know much more about Persepolis. You damned amateur!' he cried.

Heynes turned to me: 'He's always like this. He doesn't understand that we have to start all over again from the *beginning*!' He was sitting on the floor surrounded by his North–South plans.

'Listen,' I said to Richard, 'if the professor decides to publish then he'll certainly use your plans.'

'Certainly,' affirmed Heynes, 'and in any case, he'll pay no attention to my "amateur" plans. We can drink a vodka to that.'

Reconciled, we drank another vodka.

'And Barbara?' I asked.

'She didn't want to go near vodka from the sugar factory,' claimed Heynes.

'And he should know,' Richard said drowsily.

'I've never heard of her not going near *any* kind of vodka,' I said. I knew Barbara and was worried.

But Heynes no longer replied. I put my glass down by my deckchair and went out. The door was just a frame with a mosquito net stretched across it. The sensation was familiar, pushing aside the thin partition that separated a room filled with peaceful, lamplit warmth from the great surrealism that lay outside—the moonlight, the gleam of the desert, the strips of ground you could cross up to the starkly white, rocky ridges, the place of royal tombs where ibex spent the night and foreign ships with paralysed sails lay for eternity.

It wasn't cold but the lukewarm air made me shiver. I walked between the empty flowerbeds dug by the new director's wife, a woman from the American Midwest. Then came the sites of broken remains just like in our garden in Rages. There was the pomegranate orchard— the memory of its shadow, which accompanied me to my bedroom along a brook in which tarantulas swam, was almost homely. And outside, past the yellow garden walls, the bells of the camel caravans could be heard . . .

There was nothing here, just an expanse of undefiled earth—Persepolis. And moonlight across the sloping rocky ridges. I looked for Barbara. I walked carefully between the sites of remains and, when they ended, over sand drifts. Then I stumbled over the rails of a track and up a freshly dug mound of earth. Behind it was the garage with a Buick and two old Ford trucks.

'Barbara!' I shouted. She was sitting high up, almost in the shadow of the rocks. 'What makes you come all the way out here?' she asked. 'Couldn't you sleep without me? It's a decent time for going to bed!'

The moonlight lay on her feet like water lapping at the sand in waves and trickling back. I didn't say anything, I was just so happy to have found Barbara. I sat, my head resting on her bent knees, watching as the little waves rose to her feet.

NIGHTS IN RAGES,
OR THE BEGINNING OF FEAR

But those were easy nights in Persepolis. They were brightly lit, not always by the Milky Way and not always by the moonlight which flowed across the sleeping plain like a river, but by bright, light, sad conversations and by bright, light intoxicating vodka. There were long dawns that you waited for while you sat on the terrace, and there were soft breezes across hot temples. Stretched out on a camp bed, you dreamt of future paths, winding through unknown plains and heading towards mountains of hope. Reverently, you lay there, quite agitated with a desire that soared tenderly upwards like the white pillars outside, and up there, joy and sadness met—you could bear it all with a smile.

I have known quite different nights in Persia when everything lay in darkness and there was no way out. In Rages, the lifeless town next to Teheran that was only separated from the city gates by a cloud of dust, there were nights empty of friendly voices but full of alien noises. The dust cloud that divided us from the bustling capital with its lively streets was almost impenetrable because the land that it covered and shrouded was no ordinary land— it had been a site of ruins for centuries. Ever since the attack by the Mongols, no one had settled there; and no matter where you dug, you found remains of walls, fragments and traces of great destruction.

Sand covers it, carried over from the great salt desert, the last home of wild mules. Sand, despite its similarity to water and the play of waves, is a dead element. But far worse than all this—where the living no longer want to settle, the dead are buried. Hence, the strip of land between Rages and Teheran has become a vast cemetery. Mounds of sand heaped on the graves, lengthways like the corpses beneath them; small adobe gravestones; and, less frequently, a blue cupola gleaming illusively in the sun.

In the evenings when the sun has nearly set, in the distance, between the oasis trees you can make out the cupola of Shah Abdul Azim, the only glint of promise in this barren expanse. But whoever ends up on the road between the two cities at this dead hour is exposed to the closeness of death and it wouldn't take much for him to bury his face in the dust and surrender to a long sleep like one freezing to death.

Sometimes, flocks of vultures can be seen huddled far off—they wait, motionless, and their bare necks have the reddish-yellow colour of sand. The sight of the first row makes you shudder; but soon there are many more and they multiply as quickly as dreadful images in a nightmare. Soon the whole fading plain is covered with them and on the other side of the street lie nothing but graves, and dark, veiled women who bustle among the dead in shapes of grief. This sight is no less terrible; it is hardly worth averting one's eyes and making the awful choice between the two.

At the borders of the cemetery—unless it simply stretches out into infinity—camels walk from Teheran to Varamin along one of the oldest caravan trails in Persia. It goes through Rages, close by our expedition house, through the ford in front of the gates and along the length of our garden wall. Hence, the clanging of caravan bells is clear during the long nights in Rages; it is one of the clearest sounds in my memory. The bells sway on the camels' flanks and clang or jingle at their throats. It's a foreign sound, very distant but always with the same sorrow.

Early in the morning, a similar bell rang to wake us. The dogs that liked sleeping next to my bed on a straw mat awoke with a start. And another day began. I hardly had time to throw on my trousers, shirt and leather waistcoat. Gellina, an old Russian woman, stood in front of the door with a glass of tea in her hand. 'Drink, my child,' she said. She never called me anything but 'her child', and when I returned to Rages a year later she embraced me in tears. It was said that, before she came to Rages as a maid, she had run a brothel in Teheran. But what did that matter? She was good-hearted and tender, and a poor soul. She often told me that she prayed for my soul every night. And I was in need of it.

The bell sounded at four o'clock during the hot months and in the autumn at five. The autumn dawn was a continuation of the night. An amazing spectrum of light moved across the pale sky. We drove out in a truck to the excavation site where our workers were performing their morning prayers towards the east. Sometimes it was bitterly cold but by eight o'clock, when the breakfast bell sounded, the sun would have reached our tent and as we ate, we'd be taking off our leather waistcoats. The mornings at the excavation site were long, the days short. It got dark in the museum as we sat on stools, ordering objects and drawing catalogue numbers.

Beside me was George, my best friend. Later, the other workers were allowed to go home but we sat all day in the museum and 'finished up'. There was a lot to do. That was when Vann began drinking and sitting at his plotting board at night. That is how we got used to working after our evening meal too. Each of us had a petroleum lamp on our desks. I typed catalogue cards. George had a more difficult and scientific task—he had to look at coins under a microscope. The director sat, a batch of objects spread before him, writing in the large catalogue book from which I made a short transcript for the cards. The director was a hard-working German; he drank little, didn't read at all and worked a lot. His wife, a rich, young American, sometimes came into the museum and treated us to vodka. We drank as we worked, shivering. That's how the long evenings passed.

Through the pomegranate orchard, George accompanied me to my room. Although we never spoke about it, he knew I was afraid of the walk. My fear was un-founded and strange. I'd survived greater dangers on my own than walking through an orchard that belonged to an American expedition team, surrounded by a high adobe wall. That's why the Russian, Bibenski, didn't understand I was afraid; he thought I was a brave girl.

Some evenings, after work, I sat in his barracks and smoked a hashish pipe with him. We sat on the *pisé* floor, our backs leaning against the wall. Sometimes he gave me a cushion and a posteen, sometimes he forgot. His servant filled our pipes—a chunk of yellowish, clay-coloured hashish powder, and over it a layer of tobacco. Bibenski, gaunt, with prominent cheekbones and dully gleaming, feverish eyes, breathed in deep lungfuls. I couldn't. I choked and coughed. The servant Hassan, a fifteen-year-old boy, watched me and laughed. The Russian knelt in front of me, opened his lips, breathed in deeply and forced me to do the same. I copied him, coughing, until everything spun round.

'You'll never learn,' he said.

'I'd rather go to bed,' I said, and went out into the garden. It was quiet there . . . But in front of the museum door, in the shadows, George was waiting. 'I'll come with you,' he said, silently guessing my nameless fear. Fear? Back then, I didn't even realize what that new feeling was. Later, when it overwhelmed me and almost pulled me under, I understood. And, since then, a nameless fear has hung like a plume of smoke over the great, colourful desert of this country, above my sometimes blissful and sometimes terrible memories of it.

Our garden was the pomegranate orchard of a rich Persian. Among the short trees lay our site of remains, and next to the path flowed the murky brook full of tarantulas. Beyond it stood the adobe walls that separated us from the outside world. But what did 'outside world' mean? The dust cloud, the caravan trail, the ford, the cemetery plain, the vulture plain, the dust-shrouded road to the capital?

We knew that under the sand lay ruins and we were digging for precious remains. But that belonged to the day. And now it was night-time.

George walked along the avenues with me; the large, spotted dogs that slept next to my bed and chased off rats kept us company.

Gellina was asleep on the terrace. I took a petroleum lamp from the table before I went into my room. George said goodnight and his firm handshake reassured me for a moment. 'You needn't be afraid,' he said, and his torch slid over the steps and down into the dark garden. Sometimes we went up to the roof and smoked. At our feet and along the garden wall lay the river. It shimmered silver and ran through the plain towards the Damavand. You could follow it for miles but it was no real comfort. There is no true comfort in such countries. And I always believed that perished fish floated downstream on the water's silvery surface, their silver bellies turned upwards . . .

Then I lay on my bed and above me were beams with straw in between, and the spotted dogs breathed peacefully beside me, looking up for a moment when I moved. The night of dreams began. The wall of the little house, the wall of my room, was the continuation of the garden wall; and even if it protected me against wind and autumn rain, it didn't protect me from the clanging of the caravan bells, the cries of the drivers, herding the camels through the ford, or the slow murmuring of the silver river. There was no protection against these things. Nothing could be done to stop them and I wept for my mother.

As though a mortal soul could have heard me.

Slowly I began to understand. This was the beginning of the fear. And I can never get over it, never forget it.

THREE TIMES IN PERSIA . . .

I have tried to live in Persia in every way. I haven't managed to. All about me I saw people trying to live too. They fought the same dangers. As long as the dangers were real, everything was fine. Like me, they survived the long mountain paths, the nights beside flooded riverbanks, the attacks of exhaustion and demoralization. Like me, they returned to the capital city some day, lived in embassies, bathed, ate well and rose late.

They believed as I had that in this way they could restore their health and prepare for new adventures. They survived dysentery and fever, they began to drink, they went out every night for weeks on end to the cheerless bars in Teheran where there was whisky and music and dancing. Life went on like in any European city. Some day you roused yourself . . . but how long would it last? Because then came the moment of intangible danger—moral resolutions could no longer be made, and pulling yourself together no longer worked.

The danger has various names. Sometimes it's called homesickness; sometimes it's the arid, high-altitude wind that tugs at your nerves; sometimes it's the alcohol, sometimes worse poisons. Sometimes it has no name . . .

During the first months, I travelled with new friends and became familiar with everything—Persepolis and Isfahan, the garden of Shiraz, the dervish hermitages in the bare rock face, the great mosque gates, the endless streets, the endless plains. I drove through passes and rode along the bridle paths in the Elburz Mountains. I saw the shores of the Caspian Sea, jungles and paddy fields, zebus standing on sand-swept beaches, straw roofs in the heavy rain, Turkmen loggers and shepherds, and the great empty squares in the market towns of Rasht and Babol. I saw the richness of Mazandaran, the epitome of melancholy.

I left Persia from the harbour of Pahlavi. I spent the whole day there. Camel caravans wearing bells trailed in from Tabriz through the misty grey streets. Taxi drivers waited in front of hotels for travellers coming from Baku. In the courtyard of the guesthouse, I met a man who looked like a tired, malaria-infected, European explorer. He recognized me though I couldn't remember where we'd met. He called himself Shanghai Willy and was a Danish engineer.

'I'm leaving,' I said, 'and won't be coming back.'

'That's what they all say,' he claimed.

We had a drink together and then it was time and he accompanied me over to the customs building. A customs officer told me that the ship was to be loaded with a cargo of rice and so wouldn't leave until seven o'clock in the evening. We walked up and down, smoking among the piles of goods. But smoking was forbidden in the customs house and outside. So we hired a boat and were rowed out into the lagoon. We could see the little harbour from there and the Russian ships that were in fact very small steamships, looked to us like giants. At the narrowest part of the lagoon, the first pillars of a bridge could be made out.

'That's what I'm building,' said Shanghai Willy, proudly. I had to listen to how the workers were lowered in waterproof tanks to excavate holes for the buttresses. I had to listen to a great deal about the bridges that Shanghai Willy had built in Turkey and Iraq. What he'd done in China for eight years he didn't say. We were rowed back to shore and docked at his house. We had to climb over beams and concrete blocks to finally reach the stairs.

In the house above, Nils sat a drawing desk, his twenty-year-old Swedish assistant with reddish skin, a shock of blond hair, and a large child's mouth.

'Get us a drink,' said his boss.

Nils stood up and nodded, then went into the room next door and came back with glasses, and a half-empty whisky bottle. Shanghai Willy raised the bottle and scrutinized it against the lamplight.

'You didn't drink all that last night?' he asked.

'I certainly did,' said Nils.

We drank the other half of the bottle. From time to time, I went over to the window and looked over to the harbour mole where my steamship lay.

'When it starts to give off smoke, it's still early enough to leave,' said Nils.

We reached the bridge at the last minute; Shanghai Willy and Nils stood on the waterfront, their hands in their pockets. For a little way, a pilot boat bearing the Persian flag accompanied us out.

That's how I left Persia the first time.

Four months later, I came back from Russia and landed again in Pahlavi. But I have already spoken about that; the day was overcast. Afterwards, I lodged in Rages in the pomegranate garden. It wasn't a bad way to live at the time—we worked a great deal, and our Islamic and Chinese pottery shards absorbed us so completely that the sound of the caravan bells barely reached our ears. Even the dead land between the neighbouring cities was far from our thoughts. Only during the long nights did it all come to life, and then I could hardly tell it apart from my dreams. Slowly, the dream world took a violent hold of me; even more slowly, the fear. And then I began to grasp the deadly size of this country that enchanted us every morning with its beauty and supernatural sunrise.

That was my second attempt to live in Persia. When I left Rages shortly before Christmas, it hadn't been decided which of us would return. But we didn't talk about it. In the last days, we packed thirty crates for museums in Boston and Philadelphia; they had paid for our excavations in return for Islamic ceramics. We packed bowls that were painted with cobalt and lustre, and older receptacles made of heavy earthenware that were stippled or had overrun glazes. They were inaccurately referred to as *gabri* or 'wares of the fire-worshippers'. Then there were large, flat white bowls, Chinese imitations, and others with turquoise-green stripes on black backgrounds. We used up enormous amounts of wood wool and newspaper and wrote the addresses with red pens on the sealed crates. Fragments of pottery were packed too, each given a catalogue number and then an index was made for every crate.

The museum was too small; we packed in the open air, in the icy autumn wind.

One day, George went off with the two trucks. No one envied him the job of transporting thirty crates across the mountains and through the Syrian Desert to the Mediterranean.

Then the expedition broke up quickly. As soon as we reached Teheran, we lost contact, as though we'd never walked together in the early morning across the excavation site of Rages . . .

Exactly four months later, I returned to the Orient and went ashore in Beirut. Before the expedition, I'd heard nothing, I didn't even know when work in Rages would start again.

Even before driving over to the hotel, I went to the customs house to ask about my car. There, among the many crates and bales of fabric, I met my friend George again.

It was nothing more than a coincidence, and we soon parted as we both had our affairs to sort out.

In the evening, George came to my hotel and we drank a cocktail on the terrace. He told me he was going to be the deputy director in Rages, and that he'd brought two new Buicks along. An aeroplane was due to arrive soon too. By chance, my new car was also a Buick. George was short of time, he had to take the shortest route via Baghdad; but I, on the other hand, had a long journey ahead that would take me via Mosul through Kurdistan and up to the Russian border. That's a nice plan, said George, and was envious. I don't know why but, even as we talked about it, I suddenly felt demoralized.

It was quite hot in Beirut at the time, and we were glad of the night wind that came in from the sea. We drank another cocktail and I promised to pick up George from his hotel the next day. Then we would try out my new Buick on the asphalt coastal road.

But it never came to that. When I asked after George, he'd already left for Damascus.

It wasn't that important as I was to meet him a few weeks later in Teheran. In any case, it'd been a coincidence that we'd met at all in the customs house in Beirut. Despite this, the same feeling of demoralization dogged me for a long time and I told myself it might be simply due to the 'coincidence' of our encounter. What if I'd asked George to take me with him? I knew he wouldn't have minded. But I hadn't asked him and now it was too late. I reflected on how coincidence plays such a great—if deceptive—role in those countries where we seem to move with such unlimited freedom. Once again, I'd chosen my path for very arbitrary reasons. The detour to Kurdistan? Where was it I was really trying to get to?

And today I find myself in this valley, the 'Happy Valley', the valley that lies at the end of all paths.

THE BEGINNING OF SILENCE

Sometimes I wonder why I write down all these memories. Would I want to give them to strangers to read? Would I want to put myself in their hands or, if not theirs, then loved ones or good friends? But what would I be letting slip? I am certain that this book doesn't have any confidential material.

My English acquaintances sometimes ask me what I'm writing. 'An impersonal diary,' I answer. Because nothing could be more impersonal than to describe this valley—a painter would understand it better—or the mountain ranges and plains and roads and rivers. Even if I write how we lived during our expedition, it is still a long way from a personal confession. The nights on the terrace of Persepolis? The drunken conversations? Our occasional tipsiness and Bibenski's hashish pipe? That's no more personal than the melancholy earth of Mazandaran, or the shrill whistle of the Russian steam-ship in the harbour of Pahlavi. And it might be just as impersonal in the early morning to spot the delicate cloud round the shimmering peak of the Damavand, and to recognize it, one night, in the shadow of the tent, an unreal substance round the stern shoulders of an angel . . .

So it's not that I wonder why I'm revealing myself but rather why I write at all. Because it is certainly not easy to do—it's a terrible and probably fruitless toil. One has to *remember*, and, even if a memory doesn't free me for a moment, nor my companions, we don't need to know about it. We're already used to being in the state peculiar to this country—we are never free, not for a moment. We're not 'ourselves', the unfamiliar takes hold of us and makes strangers of our own hearts.

At first, we call it 'taking in intense impressions'. We abandon ourselves to the power of the landscape, its wonderful colours and pure shapes, its regal character. We detect alien creatures, first with curiosity, shortly afterwards with resistance. But we forget that this resistance will not stay with us for long.

The robust laughingly shrug off the temptations that creep up stealthily, like a disease. The clever go home in time. But many are too weak and I am the weakest of them all.

I have written about this country for a long time in the most objective way, without revealing myself at all. So where does this bitter urge to confess come from? Can I confide in none of my friends? Do those who live here not have any advice? Can't they help?

But, strange as it sounds, we shy away from saying how things really are. We often talk about Persia, and it is surely worth talking about its wonders and peculiarities.

But if someone is homesick, he doesn't mention it. And that is merely the first step in suffering.

If I were at home, on some friendly European shore, I would have faith in the possibility of an enlightening chat—the kind that doctors expect so much from—but no one here believes in anything whatsoever. The angels are too strong, and they walk on unharmed feet; people do not want to trouble one another. One never quite knows where others are weak—perhaps in the same spot? And so silence descends. One calls it toughening up . . .

Part Two

An Attempt in Love

THE ACCUSAL

I want to describe an episode that was beautiful and ordinary, something that includes the words 'love' and 'happiness', and that nearly saved us, myself and another girl, from the fate that she suffered not long after. The fact that I couldn't save her—although she'd put hope in me—added greatly to my final demoralization.

The girl's name was Jalé. Her mother was Circassian, and her father was an old man, one of those orthodox and respectable Turks who is loath to accept the changes taking place in his homeland.

I've already mentioned Jalé and her younger half-sister, Zadikka. I even let myself get carried away at the start of these notes to recount that, when the heat was white and deadly across Teheran's plains, I pulled into the Turk's shadowy garden, and felt comforted, almost rescued. Yes, it was a comfort and a shelter! I could breathe again!

But why did so much time have to pass until I found my way there? Later on, I could find my way whether in darkness or in daylight, and I even knew the tree roots that stuck out on the last corner. It became my daily route—and then I wasn't allowed to take it any more. I'd obviously tried to turn it into something everyday; I'd felt so sure as though it had become reality. But it took bitter revenge.

It was then that I realized you can't afford to get caught up in any emotion in this country, and you can't rely on any hope that threatens to break up the path of despair. I'd almost come to accept this when I met Jalé. It was true that I woke up every morning in a shadowy, dark, ancient Persian garden, but this did nothing to alter the fact that, every morning, I was overcome by the trepidation of being faced by a force (like the day before and the day before that) for which my limited strength was no match. Again and again, I was assaulted by this country, this sky, this great plain and its mountainous edges—where to run to? There was no shelter, no sigh of relief . . .

So when Jalé arrived I didn't want to believe at first that such a simple, tender comfort was possible between two people. And when it was snatched away from us, I would have felt that even this heartache was justified although the brutal justice of the non-human world is bitter and incomprehensible—but there was no protest against it. Instead, much worse than all this—it was not something powerful, huge and incomprehensible that made my attempts futile and my comfort worthless—it was merely an uncaring stranger who came between us and did me harm. This is a country where you have no enemies, and your friends aren't capable of much. Even the person nearest to you doesn't realize that you're suffering and struggling to breathe—you are alone. So why the need for animosity? Why would a person hate another or cause him pain that lies beyond all possibility. Why quarrel? Don Quixote could attack windmills, they roused his courage; but there was nothing to attack, nothing to fight for, and no one could envy another, not even his enemies!

I know that all this will be resolved one day. Jalé's death and my desperately errant life—both will be made accountable and I won't protest against what has been done to me. I have only one accusal that is more bitter than any other—uncaring strangers came between us and did me harm . . .

JALÉ

When Jalé and I saw one another for the first time, I was running a fever. My room was darkened by the old trees and thick bushes in the garden. It was five o'clock in the evening, a hot day in July. I was lying on my bed, shaking from the chills and waiting for the fever. Jalé was pale; the blue powder on her eyelids made her eyes seem even bigger, her forehead even whiter. Artificial rouge lay like a sickness on her prominent cheekbones.

I'd heard that she had lung disease. As a child, she'd stayed in Davos with her mother. Then came the World War and her young and very beautiful mother left her husband. He made the little girl pay for it—she was sent to school in Turkey and was not allowed to see her mother again.

Turkey was poor then, a country devastated by war, fighting a heroic battle for its liberation. Jalé's father was poor too, and the school was poor, and the children didn't have enough to eat. Jalé's mother asked if she could take the child—she had a rich lover. But the father's honour was more important to him than Jalé's already-too-frail life. Jalé believed she would soon die without seeing her mother again.

In the meantime, Kemal Pasha, a turbulent, hardened patriot, had won his first battles from his base in the Anatolian steppe. The Greeks in Smyrna were murdered; soon afterwards, the English withdrew and the persecution of the Armenians began. The brave Kurds rose up in their mountains but were soon forced into submission by Kemal Pasha.

Jalé's mother had her daughter kidnapped from school and brought to her lover's house, a poet who stood in the dictator's favour. Jalé said that those were her happiest years. But then her disease broke out again and the girl had to be taken to a sanatorium—not in Switzerland this time but near Stambul—and later, her father took her with him to Teheran.

He had a new wife, and, from her, his most beautiful daughter, Zadikka. Nevertheless, he didn't want to let his older daughter go. He would never forgive Jalé that his first lover left him. He would never forgive her that the Circassian was young and beautiful when he already felt old. He would never forgive her that her young mother didn't love him, didn't respect his honour and left him for another.

He probably loved Jalé, who looked like her mother. But he made her pay for this love, and it looked like hatred.

'Is there nothing I can do for you?' Jalé asked me.

'It'll pass,' I said. My teeth were chattering from the chills and I knew that I would have to press my knees together and clutch my pillow tightly, and that the pain in my back would get worse until it was unbearable. But there was no need to be embarrassed in front of Jalé. My hand lay in her long, cool fingers.

'The fever will come soon,' she said.

'Yes,' I said, 'then everything will get better. Then I'll dream.'

I looked at her. I already found her exceptional presence comforting.

CONVERSATION ABOUT HAPPINESS

She once said to me, 'You have to think of life, even if I'm thinking of something completely different.'

'What are you thinking of?' I asked.

'Something quite different, quite far away.'

'Why can't I know?'

She smiled. 'Because I don't want to tell you. Because you have malarial fever, but it'll pass. My sickness won't pass. It's carrying me away, like a river.'

'And I'm supposed to think of life?'

'Because I can't. We have quite different things in store.'

'We'll both end up in this country,' I said.

'Don't you understand?' she asked softly, 'This country doesn't hurt me any more. Not even my father can hurt me.'

'But Jalé,' I said, 'he's doing you wrong. If only he'd let you leave and go to a country with purer, better air, if only he'd let your mother look after you again . . .'

'Then we'd have a similar path,' she said. 'Then, my darling, we could think of the same things and I wouldn't be afraid of dragging you over to my side.'

'Yes, then we wouldn't need to be afraid of anything.'

'Why are you afraid?'

'You know why. I'm never happy.'

We contemplated what the word 'happiness' meant and why some have it in store and it eludes others for a lifetime.

'Perhaps one has to fight for it,' I said, 'but there are so many other things one has to fight for, and it's an invisible opponent.'

'Opponent?'

'People say they long for happiness. But something unknown, far away, which you can't imagine . . . ?'

'Can't you imagine it?'

'Can you?'

'It's a silver river,' said Jalé, 'and it carries me between its banks which I am impervious to and that can't stop me.'

'The hills draw back.'

'And become a plain.'

'First you hear the wind—it chases the clouds like a flock of wild ducks across the river.'

'Their shadows skim the water, and I feel a chill. But then the wind stops and the river becomes calm. The wind disappears up on the plain and evening falls.'

'Jalé!'

She didn't hear me. She was thinking of something far, far away.

We had wanted to talk about happiness and didn't notice that we were thinking about death . . .

SOMEONE WILL COME BETWEEN US

We had many conversations together. We wanted to talk about nothing special and made no effort to say important things. We had nothing we wanted to make clear, and we had no need to get to know one another.

'Perhaps I'm not the girl you think I am,' said Jalé once. 'Perhaps I'm quite different.'

'I don't think you're anything,' I answered.

'Perhaps you'd be disappointed.'

But that was all that was said and there was no reason for me to be disappointed in any way since I didn't think about Jalé much, and even less about my relationship to her. There was the path from my house to hers—the path with the tree roots that stuck out on the final corner—and that, even if it was taken for granted and ordinary, was enough. In the afternoon, we lay in the shade of the big tree and talked while young people, who were guests in the Turk's garden, played tennis across from us. There were some nice people among them, and we sometimes sat by the tennis court and watched them. But the bright light made Jalé tired, and everyone got used to leaving us alone under our tree. Neither of us, in any case, was allowed to play.

Towards the evening, Jalé's father came home from the office. He got out of the car and went straight to the tennis court. As he passed us, he greeted me and said a few words to Jalé. He had a quiet, very hard voice, and it was enough to make Jalé sad.

Her fever came back and he scolded her because of it.

'He wants me to go to the tennis court and look after the guests,' she said.

'Can't he see that you're ill?'

'He said if I were ill I wouldn't be able to talk to you either. Then I'd have to stay in my room.'

'Shall we go to your room? Perhaps it's better if you lie down?'

Her face took on an expression of dejected suffering, such that I was less able to bear than if she'd wept. 'No,' she said, 'I can't breathe in there. It makes me afraid. And he wouldn't let you stay with me!'

'Doesn't he know that you enjoy my company?'

'He hates everything that makes me happy. He doesn't want my life to be easier.'

It was only then that I realized what we were up against.

'Don't let it make you sad,' said Jalé. She turned my head and looked at me. 'My mother would love you,' she said.

We both smiled.

'In the end, he can't separate us,' I said.

'He can't stop me loving you,' said Jalé.

'No,' I said, 'he can't separate us.'

She held my head in her hands as if to placate me. 'He can,' she said. 'That's exactly what he can do. And that's exactly what he's going to do.'

'Jalé!'

'Don't be angry with me that I told you.'

'Jalé, doesn't he know that we only have one another and nothing else? Why would he want to cause us so much heartache?'

'He's going to do it soon,' said Jalé softly.

A GARDEN PARTY

I saw Jalé again when I returned to the city from the Lar Valley. This fact shows me, to my surprise, that I must have broken up my stay. It's a chronological fact and only goes to show how little influence what we call reality has on us. Because no matter how carefully I trace events in my memory, our first farewell was final, and, from the moment we first mounted the mules in Abala and arrived in this valley via the two passes, I knew this to be my final path and this camp to be my last stay. It might as well have been a caravan procession for the dead that moved along, its bells ringing softly, in the glare of the Persian summer. But I've only ever seen such caravans in the Iraqi desert, camels bearing long, narrow coffins on their flanks, or the dead wrapped in nothing but a carpet and being taken, in accordance with their devout wishes, to Karbala or Najaf, the holy burial place of the Shi'ites. Such trips often took thirty days and the graves in the holy areas were expensive. But what a comfort it was to have a last wish, and to soothe poor souls in fulfilling it; because no matter how much one might have erred in life, now, for once, the way ahead was mapped out.

I especially think about the camel drivers and caravan guides. Although the routes that they follow have been the same since time immemorial, sandstorms still sweep across the tracks and make them unrecognizable; storms wash the last remains away, and in spring, rivers with secret sources fill the dry fords whose slopes are otherwise homes to snakes and lizards and a peril for bare feet. When the conditions are like this, the Bedouins stand in front of their flapping tents and no longer know where the sun sets; the prayers that leave their lips are torn to shreds and don't reach Allah's ears, and even the best caravan guide can get lost. He makes his camels lie in a circle and they hunker down until the storm lets up; their long necks sink until their heads touch, like a wheel.

After so many risks and errant ways, I think to myself, the last wish of a pious camel driver is understandable. For he can be sure that the caravan procession of the dead will reach the green oasis of Karbala or the white city of Najaf that glitters like a fata morgana in the desert, surrounded by a broad belt of graves and crowned by the golden cupola of its mosques.

So, once again I saw the road leading from Abala. The ascents seemed longer, the descents steeper and the depths of the furrows in the dead valley even more lifeless, its water motionless, this time not even stirred by a bird's heartbeat.

When at last we were driving along the main road, we saw in the distance a hazy mist across the plain; it was the dust enveloping the city of Teheran like a poisonous cloud.

That same evening, the Foreign Minister gave a reception. Hundreds of lights illuminated the bushes, their leaves suffocated by fine layers of dust, and perforated Persian lamps hung lifelessly over the elaborately designed paths. The deadly violence of summer reigned over the celebration.

Next to me sat the German chargé d'affaires, a man who'd been living in Persia for six years and loved it. He died that very night from a heart attack.

Two hundred guests were invited and were sauntering among the groves and the two open galleries of the house from which wide steps led down into the garden. Above played a European band. From where I was sitting, I could see the dancers—men and women dressed in white with mask-like faces, blonde coiffures and smooth partings. They danced some distance apart, the women placing their hands on their partners' shoulders as if quietly resisting them.

It was late when I saw Jalé and her appearance gave me a strangely acute pain. Since the last time I had seen her, she looked even sicker.

Up on the gallery, the music stopped. I could suddenly hear nothing but the people's voices next to me.

As if through a narrow alley, Jalé came towards me, surrounded by other young girls. The alley was a path between dark bushes, the small lamps throwing their dim light on Jalé's very pale, heavily made-up face. I gauged the distance between us—it wasn't far.

Had I sometimes invoked this face when I was up in the valley, I wondered? But I'd only spoken to an angel, and remembering his quiet presence in the shadows of my tent, I became aware of my terrible loneliness.

Jalé stopped some way off and chatted, her soft voice carrying over to me. Despite the pain in my infected leg, I stood up and went towards her.

'You're back early,' she said.

'Not because of the party.'

She looked at me.

'And not for you,' I said softly, 'It's because of this infection. I need to see a doctor. That's the only reason,' I added, as though it were necessary to throw suspicion miles away.

'Who's going to bring you back up there?'

'Yes,' I said, 'I'll be going back as soon as possible.'

'Of course,' she said, placatingly.

'And you're feverish . . .' I looked at her white face, the patchy redness of the sickness on her cheeks, and I didn't recognize my own voice when I asked, 'Couldn't I stay here? Couldn't I do something for you?'

'Come with me,' she said.

We went up to the gallery alone. I supported myself on the handrail.

'You can hardly walk,' said Jalé, suddenly concerned.

'Yes, it burns like hellfire,' I said laughing.

We looked out over the balustrade and down into the garden. The red lamps were swaying now in the barely perceptible night wind.

'It's getting cooler,' said Jalé. The coolness was nothing more than a small lungful of air; beyond the garden, the poisonous cloud still hung, smouldering above the roofs that were incandescent with heat.

'My father won't let me see you any more,' Jalé said abruptly. 'He won't let me see anyone.'

The dancers started up again; their bodies were far apart and they moved slowly past me. Although I'd known this for a long time, a bewildering fear seized me.

'Please don't take it like this,' said Jalé, near me.

But she was already far away. It was as though we were dancing like the others, slowly and without hope, to escape the festive night all round us.

'He knows I'm sick now. He doesn't want to lose me. That's why he's cut me off from everyone. He's stubborn.'

'Can't you go to your mother's?'

Then I saw she was fighting back tears. She was arched backwards over the railing, breathing deeply to brace herself against weakness, fever and the violence of tears.

'Don't take on so,' I said.

'You were already so far away,' she replied. 'It was a last goodbye!'

I wanted to protest, grasp her hands, accuse.

'You'd only set him against me,' said Jalé, very softly, as though there was no harm being done to her, to us. 'He'd think I was setting my friends against him for support. His pride couldn't cope with that. He'd take his revenge on me and it wouldn't help you at all. And now I have to go.'

I saw her go down the steps, amid the many guests who were walking up and down, then into the garden, then no more.

WHISKY, FEVER AND SINGING WORKERS

The doctor merely glanced at my leg the next day, by then swollen to the hip. 'Couldn't you have come earlier?' he asked.

'It wasn't that easy,' I said. 'It's a long way.'

'You've got a fever too, a pretty high fever.'

'I don't mind the fever.'

'But you'll mind when I have to cut into this infected lump of flesh.'

I was used to this way of dealing with patients. I was used to English doctors in the tropics. 'Well,' he said, 'don't get worked up. Drink a stiff whisky first.' He stood up and fetched a bottle from a shelf on the wall. 'I'll drive you to the hospital afterwards,' he said. He poured some whisky into a glass. 'I'm afraid I can't offer you any ice,' he said, 'I've got nothing against bacteria, but enough is enough. And clear summer ice from Teheran would simply kill a person with your lack of resistance.'

Afterwards we went to his car. I couldn't put any weight on my infected foot.

'From the bungalow to your car feels like seven miles,' I said.

He gripped below my shoulders to support me. 'I knew that whisky would work wonders,' he said. 'You can still walk in a straight line.'

When I awoke from the anaesthetic, I said, 'Everything I said was a lie. I want Jalé to come.'

'We've already sent for her,' said the nurse, 'and we've already taken off the bandage.'

'You're a nice girl,' I said, 'but you don't need to believe everything I said.'

'Of course not,' said the nice girl, 'we just took the bandage off because you insisted on it and we've written the letter you dictated.'

'I never dictated a letter!'

'It was only a short letter. And your friend will soon be here to visit you.'

It was a long, hot night. I looked at my leg on the white linen and my foot on the pillow. It was no longer a lump but the wound burned and my foot felt as though it wasn't part of me.

Early in the morning, the workers began to sing. They were building a house and I could see the scaffolding from my window. Persian workers build a house in a few days—they pile blocks of damp, unfired clay and sing as they work. The foreman sings, 'Give me a brick. Give me half a brick, a whole brick . . .' Sometimes he shouts at a boy below who passes up the adobe bricks: 'Can't you hear, you idiot, you son of a dog!' That's the only variation. Then he continues singing in his equanimous way: 'Half a block, and now a whole one.'

After a few hours, I began to shout. The nice nurse came in. 'I'm sorry,' I said, 'I can't move otherwise I'd have rung for you.'

'You shouldn't shout so loudly. The patient in the next room has typhoid fever.'

'Sorry . . .'

'The doctor won't be here till one o'clock. He has to embalm the German.'

I felt nausea rising.

'It's just the heat,' said the girl.

'Please,' I said, 'could you just ask the people outside to stop singing?'

She left. The workers carried on singing until sunset. Jalé didn't come.

The following night, I began a conversation with the nurse. 'How can you work in this heat?' I asked.

'You get used to it. As long as you're healthy . . .'

'Do you think I'll ever get better?'

She smiled. 'If only we had easy cases like you all the time!'

'You mean, as long as people don't have typhoid fever?'

'No, I didn't mean that. People die easily out here, from all kinds of things. But just look at your foot.'

'It looks quite healthy.'

'Except for the cut. In a few days, you'll be able to dance again.'

'If only it was just about dancing!'

'Hasn't the doctor told you you'll be discharged in a couple of days?'

'If only it was just about *that*!'

'So what is it you're afraid of then?' asked the nice nurse.

I sat up a little. 'Listen,' I said, 'do you think I'll get better? Did you really write that letter I dictated to you?'

She put her sewing aside. 'Of course,' she said, rather disconcerted, 'of course!'

'Yes, I remember I dictated a letter to you for my friend, Jalé.'

'Do you remember now?'

'First I said I hadn't, but now I know I did. I know full well I did. I remember what it says in the letter—but as you can see,' I continued, 'she still hasn't come.'

'Perhaps she didn't have time today.'

'You don't understand. She won't come tomorrow either.'

'Couldn't you be a little more patient?'

'No,' I said, 'you don't understand. If you start being patient in this country, then you're lost!'

The nice nurse bent over me. 'You're still a little feverish. You should try and sleep.' When I didn't reply, she suddenly added, 'You mustn't be afraid of this country and blame it for anything. Don't even start doing that!

I didn't even try to be patient; for the last time, I tried to rebel. The doctor had to reopen up my wounds because they were suppurating.

'I'm so sorry I have to hurt you like this,' he said, 'but it's not worth giving you an anaesthetic.'

The nice nurse holding my foot glanced at me.

'In this heat,' said the doctor, 'you shouldn't put too much strain on your heart.'

'Didn't you treat a girl called Zadikka when she had dysentery? Do you know Zadikka's sister? Do you think that she's very sick?'

'You mean Jalé? Those Turkish girls are very used to doing what they're told. She'll be destroyed by that stubborn father of hers.'

'And she knows it . . .'

'But I can't use force. I can't just kidnap her!'

'No,' I said angrily, 'you can't even see to it that Jalé comes to visit me!'

'Try to concentrate more on your own health,' said the doctor.

'But I do have the right to see her!'

'Of course,' said the nurse, in a friendly way.

The doctor touched the cut. 'And now brace yourself,' he said.

I braced myself. He made an incision in what felt like the most sensitive part.

When the bandage was back on, they left me alone. The workers were singing; the adobe wall was growing with astonishing speed. When they've finished, they'll stop singing, I thought. But then it occurred to me that the new house would need four walls, and when all four walls were built, another house would probably be built next to it. It will carry on this way forever, I thought.

I couldn't reach the bell next to my bed and I didn't dare cry out even though the patient with typhoid fever in the room next door had died the previous night.

In the late afternoon, when the heat had cooled a little, the singing outside my window suddenly stopped.

The unfamiliar silence was almost more agonizing.

The burning in my foot eased up and I lay drowsily on the hot and damp linen sheets.

If only I could reach for the pack of cigarettes and light one, I thought, if only I could smoke, that would be a sign that I'm almost healthy again. 'I'm healthy, I'm healthy,' I heard myself saying out loud . . .

No one answered. The sweats started and it was exhausting to shout into the emptiness. It's good that no one can hear me, I thought, they'd think I was crazy. You don't just shout when you're all alone. I'm not drunk, I'm quite sober, they haven't given me anything . . .

Fearfully, I held my breath. And if they'd given me something, like morphine, I thought, then I wouldn't be shouting out loud because I wouldn't be afraid. Not afraid at all—I'd even enjoy lying here. It'd be . . . and here I began crying out again and shouting out loud . . . it'd be like a hand reaching from heaven!

At this thought, I went silent. I stretched a little, felt the creased sheet under my burning skin and calmed myself down. Someone will come soon, I said to myself; then they'll wash me with cool water and give me something to drink. Then it'll be night. Perhaps it'll be a cool night . . . I spoke quickly, so as not to let any doubts rise. Behind me, behind the paper-thin wall, fear lurked in a dark hole.

Then the nurse came in. 'You have a visitor,' she said.

As Jalé approached my bed across the dim, small room, I sat up, reached for her arms and rested my head on her shoulder.

THE FAREWELL

I didn't want to cry. It took a while until I was ready.

'I thought you'd never come,' I said, 'I was sure you'd never come.'

'I'm so sorry.'

'But you couldn't.'

'I wanted to come as soon as I got your letter. But I just couldn't.'

'It doesn't matter. I'm so happy.'

'It was so reckless of you to send me a letter.'

'I know. I realized right away that it was a mistake.'

'It wasn't a mistake, it was just reckless.'

'It's nice of you to see it that way.'

'Don't talk nonsense. Please don't talk like that!'

'But I wanted to see you at any cost. You understand, don't you, that I had to see you?'

'Yes, darling.'

'Now I can see you, now you're here . . .'

'I'm so sorry that I made you wait, my poor darling.'

'. . . and you'll never go away again. Now we'll stay together.'

She pushed me gently away and looked at me. 'Yes,' she said, 'now I'll never leave you alone again.'

'First you have to get better.'

'You too.'

'And then . . .'

She smiled at me, 'Then,' she said, 'no one can harm us any more.'

'We'll go to another country.'

'To a happy country where we're both at home.'

'Do you know where?'

'Of course,' Jalé said seriously, 'a country where no one can harm us!'

'If only you were healthy, Jalé!'

'Don't worry about me. Please don't be afraid because of me!'

'Not be afraid?' I asked.

'Not as long as I'm with you.'

'And will you always stay with me?'

'I've promised I will.'

'Yes.'

'Can't you have some faith? Don't you believe me?'

'Oh, to the end of the world . . .'

She leant towards me. 'We're already very near the end,' she said.

'But we're both still very young.'

'That doesn't matter.'

'We've been through so much pain, Jalé, and yet we're both very young. You could even say we're right at the beginning.'

'No,' she said. 'That's the least important part.'

'Doesn't it help us?'

'Darling, you mustn't think anything can help us.'

'But I believe you. I believe you to the end of the world.'

'And that makes you less afraid?'

'I think of the other country. I think that we'll be truly happy there.'

'It's good that you're not afraid. It's nice to know.'

'You just have to believe that you will truly enjoy living once again.'

'I'll always have a part of you with me.'

'But we're together, Jalé!'

'Yes,' she said softly, 'and now I must go.'

'Jalé!'

'My darling!'

'So it isn't true that you'll stay next to me?'

'No, it's not. You know very well that I can't stay.'

'Please,' I said, 'please don't leave me alone.'

'You mustn't upset yourself.'

'For God's sake, don't leave me alone.'

'God turned his back on us long ago. You shouldn't mention God now.'

'I beg you, Jalé, I beg you—'

'Be reasonable,' she said, 'if I'm not taken to hospital tomorrow, I'll come again.' She held my hands tightly and leant over me. 'Please try and hold on,' she said.

We pressed our faces together.

'Why do you think that God has turned his back on us?' I asked. 'Why are we being separated? Why do they take you away from me?'

'If only you would try and hold on,' she said. 'I can't go on. I can't help you. But if you reach another country, God and all his angels will turn to you again. If only you'll hold on.'

'I don't want to, Jalé.'

'I can't ask you for anything else, darling.' She stood up and we clasped our hands tightly again.

'Try to come back tomorrow,' I pleaded.

'Yes, my darling.'

'If only you knew how it is for me, Jalé!'

'Yes, darling.'

'You leaving and perhaps never coming back again.'

She let go of my hands gently and laid my head on the pillow. 'Our path is not much further,' she said, 'and then no one can harm us any more.'

I wanted to sit up again but she'd already reached the door.

Jalé was taken the next day to the Soviet Russian infirmary. Her father forbade any visitors, to spare her, so he said. That didn't affect me much as I couldn't even try to visit her.

My doctor told me that Jalé was so sick that only a rapid tourniquet of her left lung could save her, but she was afraid of the operation and her father wouldn't hear of it. But, in the end, I believe that even a successful operation would have granted her nothing more than a brief respite.

When my foot was almost healed, they brought me back up to the Lar Valley. I could barely remember the way this time but at some point, I was put back in my tent and everything was like it was before.

THE ANGEL AND JALÉ'S DEATH
(for Cathalene Crane)

The angel came to me a second time. I was standing in front of my tent and saw him approaching although I kept my eyes fixed on the river that had turned silver at this late hour. Between the flat and green riverbanks, it flowed undisturbed, almost noiselessly, towards the streaked cone of the Damavand. It had a long journey; black cliffs and high grassy banks would retreat, the valley would expand, and in the moonlit night, the plain would emerge.

I now knew that Jalé was going to die, and I didn't even look up to welcome the angel who stopped some distance from me.

'Do you know where this water flows?' he asked.

'No,' I said, 'but it's Jalé's water of death, and that's what it'll become overnight.'

The angel's presence disturbed me. My thoughts were with her and nothing connected me with her except for the almost noiseless current—it was as though it had reached my heart and would soon flow through me. Then I would be united with her forever even though in a mysterious way.

The angel said nothing. He was silent for so long that I forgot he was there.

When he began to speak, I started violently.

'What you are doing is sinful,' he said. 'You know very well that it will not help you and that you will never see that girl again. You know very well that no one can enter the heart of another and become as one, not even for the shortest moment. Even your mother only made you flesh, and at your first breath you breathed in solitude.'

'I know,' I said, 'but there is no comfort for us other than to love and stand by one another.'

'Can you stand by her then?' asked the angel, and his voice was quite without derision, 'Now, in her bitterest hour of need?—for she is too young to die.'

'I have to see her!' I cried, wildly. 'On a good mule, I can be on the main road in eight hours. And if I'm lucky, a car will take me to Teheran tonight.'

'You will not be allowed to go to her. You will reach the door of the infirmary perhaps, or if you are fortunate, the corridor to her room . . .'

'I'll scream!'

'Yes, you will scream and weep at your powerlessness, as people always have done: now, a hundred years ago and a thousand too, they have always rebelled, powerlessly.'

I looked at him, trembling with hatred.

'And what they call fate, and what they rebel against, is in fact nothing—a tiny obstacle in their path.'

'You're lying! You're an angel and you're deceiving me into thinking like a human being!'

The angel looked past me with a lenient expression. 'What prevents you from going to see her?' he asked. 'You know she would like to see you. Perhaps it is her only wish—perhaps she is clinging to the hope that you will enter her room tonight.'

Jalé's face swam into my vision—her white, feverishly damp forehead, the red patches of sickness on her cheeks, her beautiful, tenderly parted lips with the barely perceptible twist at the corner of her mouth that revealed her pain. And she looked at me . . . I forgot everything except for that face, it gripped me with its pain, and I asked, 'Is there no way?'

Very mildly, the angel replied, 'Her father forbids you to see her. I do not think he has good reason to do so. To tell the truth, I think his reasons are wrong and come from an embittered heart. But what does it help you to know this? He will come between you. Besides, you are very far away from her, and who can say if you will reach her in time?'

I wept. My protest was in vain. 'What have I done to that man?' I asked.

I saw the angel shake his head. The cloud that hung round his shoulders like a cloak lifted a little. And with almost human grief, he said, 'Do you not understand that you cannot reason like this? Else, you will be destroyed.

The world is full of inconceivable injustice. What did you base your hopes on? On a stranger whose heart is bitter, perhaps through no fault of his own, who takes revenge on his daughter, and comes between you? Yet, it is not impossible that he loves her. Did you not base your hopes on anything more than a stranger, the length of a night and a mule path?'

But even the path now lay in darkness. Night had fallen.

The angel had sat down on a stone on the riverbank. I saw him there; or rather, I could make out the silhouette of his figure that resembled a foreign deity, and the pale cloud of his cloak that now lay quietly in the darkness like the halo of a saint.

'She has scars on her wrist,' I said, 'because she's already tried to die. That was when she was separated from her mother.'

'And you?' asked the angel, and I recognized his harsh, ethereal voice again, 'Have you not wanted to die? What makes you think of this?'

'I simply think that it is a final exit that always remains open to us.'

'Do you have *such* a low opinion of death? Is it only good enough for you to escape from yourself?

'Not from myself but from life. It causes me too much pain. A stranger can do me such harm. Any tiny obstacle can bring me down.'

'And against such minuscule forces, you call upon the last and mightiest force to help you?'

'Don't be so unforgiving.' I said, 'you know that weak forces can bring me down. Whom should I turn to? I feel so weak that I want to give up the fight. Please don't be unforgiving—grant me permission!'

'I can neither allow nor forbid you anything. I only wish you to surrender and let yourself fall. You are almost ready.'

I leant against the tent pole. I was tired and the distance to the unmoving figure of the angel seemed to grow.

'Do you want to try and pray?' he asked, 'Have you not already tried everything else?'

'And while I pray,' I screamed, 'Jalé will die!'

'What do you still hope for?'

What did he know of Jalé's close, comforting face that had been torn away from me?

He fell silent and looked across the river towards the valley as if darkness didn't affect him.

Slowly, the cloud lifted from his shoulders, floating upwards as lightly as a feather, then slid towards the glimmering Damavand and disappeared.

The angel sat there, disrobed and motionless. 'Some weeks ago,' he said, 'you said that you were at the end of your strength. Since then, you have no longer let me support you although I came of my own accord to your tent. You prefer to cling to hope of a more human kind. Where has it led you?'

I thought I would collapse. 'Take me away from here,' I shouted—and my voice cracked, I wept loudly—'Lead my out of this valley, take me home! I want to go home!'

The angel's voice answered, 'This is my home. Did you not enter this valley of your own free will? And now you want to leave?'

Trembling with sobs, I clung to the tent pole. 'Of my own free will!' I managed to stammer, 'Ah, as an angel, do you not understand free will and us humans? Who brought me here? Why did I have to go along so many paths, why did I have to err again and again? At first, it was an adventure, then it turned into homesickness, then I began to be afraid, and no one helped me. Sure, some-one drove me away, I want to accuse, I want to make an accusation against someone, I don't want to be held responsible, I don't want to be left here alone to die, I want someone to take me home!'

I heard my exhausted voice fading away. Swiftly, it echoed back across the river, and I heard 'I want someone to take me home!'

The angel fell silent for a long time. Finally, I said quietly, wanting to ask for his forgiveness, 'Your cloud has gone!'

He smiled—I saw him smile!

'What do you care about my cloud?' he said.

And when I already believed I'd been forsaken by God and humans, even by my beloved father, I heard the angel's voice through the darkness: 'You are at the end.'

I fell silent in terror.

'You are at the end, in total darkness,' repeated the angel in his distant yet intimate way. 'Admit that, despite your youth, you have tried every path—escape routes, deviations and errant ways. You have done no harm. I believe you are no more a sinner than the next. You loved your mother. You were desperate when you were forced to realize that God does not barter and that every decision is a sacrifice. You did not even know your self and did not want to harm a soul—that is to your credit. But then you began to err. You let yourself drift to Persia, you even wanted to die—do not think you can hide anything from me. For if this is my home then I am an angel . . .'

'I came back ten times,' I interrupted, 'yet not of my free will.'

'You finally came up here,' said the angel. 'You might, in your careless way, call this "the Happy Valley" but you know that it is "the Valley at the End of the World". You have to turn back.'

'Let me die.'

'But that would not help! Have faith in me—even if you imagine Jalé's wrists—that path does not differ much from the others that have led you into my realm. Have humility. Do not think you can escape anything!'

'Of course, I know nothing of that,' I said.

'But you know,' said the angel, 'that now, tonight, you have reached the end. Give up.'

I pressed my face against the tent post.

'You are standing in a dark wood. Give up.'

'If I give up, if I want to die, can't I then pass through this wall? Won't a hole open up? Won't I fall through like a stone and be immersed in the dark waters of death over there?' I pressed my head so hard against the post that I thought it would fall over and I with it.

The angel had disappeared from my view. It was a dark night. But I knew he was still sitting there, stripped of his cloud, seated on a stone and staring towards the valley. I could even hear his ethereal voice saying: 'You are at the end but that's when help is closest to hand. Turn back.'

I don't know what Jalé went through that night. I never found out how she died. But she was alone . . .

. . . NOT MUCH TIME LEFT

I don't have much time. Summer is coming to an end, and at these heights that means leaving for good. The water level of our river is now so low that we can only catch very small fish. The white streaks on the Dama-vand's cone are thin and ragged, and the scorched vol-canic earth spreads out menacingly. But soon snow will fall and then the pyramid will put on its unearthly, lus-trous robe again, and we, unequal to this tremendous sight, will understand the sign. Perhaps only a few days are left till then? What shall we live on when snow covers the meadows again, the fish are chased off by ice or sink into a deadly slumber deep below the surface? The nomads leave, trailing past our bank, past the Afjeh Pass that leads them across two mountain ridges into a gentler valley. They trail slowly like water; black and white herds, bright-red woman's skirts, gleaming copper kettles, goat-hair felt and long tent poles, mules piled high with goods, men and boys.

I'd be able to bear this farewell with more composure and look towards the end with less apprehension if my fear wasn't so huge, leaving no room for anything else. My fear fills me, and I know that it will seize, infect and consume every other feeling.

Not only the nomads are moving to their winter quarters; the camels too, who roamed freely in the short summer along the narrow rocky ledges, looking for food among the basalt boulders, will now be herded down from their barren grazing grounds and driven to the Afjeh Pass. They will be brought to Varamin, to the great caravanserais on the famous Iranian camel market. The air is gentle there even in winter, and the fodder plentiful. But the camels know nothing of this; their freedom has made them rebellious, they break away and, with swaying gait, they trot back along the riverbank. It does them little good—they are brought back, the cries of the drivers startle them, they remember, become docile and let themselves be led along the path. Finally, an entire herd gathers where the pass slopes down; the beasts are still unsettled, still stretching their necks and rubbing their trembling flanks against one another. They seem unnaturally large, bathed in cold light, as we watch the lively herd from our camp. Then they disappear.

What are we waiting for?

Yesterday evening in the tent, we talked about our departure. Our servants are impatient, and the provisions are running out. I listened and knew that none of this applied to me any more. They asked me if perhaps I wanted to stay here and be snowed in?

But it was an unnecessary, mistaken question; that wasn't the point. Back to the lowlands? Back to the city residences of Teheran? *Back*? I can't even go forward. I've often wondered, while writing these notes, who brought me to this 'Happy Valley'? I have traced some memories back but never far enough to find the beginning.

No, no one led me here, it's no one's fault. But one thing is clear and unmistakable—the way back is ruled out, blocked by the gigantic bulk of the Damavand, soon to be cloaked in heavenly purity. Freedom only counts if one has the strength to make use of it. But I have abused it. Now Jalé has died too—seldom was someone more innocent—and what am I to do? I was much freer than she was and that's why she bore what happened to her with much less bitterness. What keeps me here now is the most terrible desperation. The hand from the heavens holds me, and it will pull me back at the right moment. That is all I am waiting for, nothing else. No departure, no return home.

I know that I won't be able to make anyone understand. Even what I have written here is utterly useless, and that occasionally distresses me. Because I fear two things: the agonizing feeling of sickness and weakness, which I can almost no longer bear; and the thought that I won't have enough time to write everything down. What I write grows less with each day; the exertion is too much. And every day I have less faith that I will be able to explain to anyone how terrible it is up here; that my suffering and fear and pain are real even if they are unfounded and seem unjustified. But it's not about that,

not that! Only those who have been in its grip can understand this. Not many things touch me now; they are too
distant, and I'd have to wear seven-league boots to reach
them. Even being alone and dying alone would not terrify
me as much if only I could somehow reach the heart of
the world and the cheerful, adventurous hearts of people
that beat towards the future, filled with hope.

Sometimes, this torturous agitation recedes and I can
breathe out, relieved, and reflect. Then I flail in all direc-
tions and no longer know which way to turn, as though
desperation were a thorny rosebush, thrashing its branches
in my face. The future is dead, not a breath of air stirs
there, no colour, no darkness, no light, and the path there
is long and too far for me to go.

I now know what stands in my way. Mountains,
deserts and sea rear up and open up before me; I have
given a lot to cross them, always carried by a hope that I
didn't want to name—for this is how we survive, through
nameless hope. Happy people swap it for destinations,
like beautifully painted pictures. But my cities are called
Constantinople, Aleppo, Baghdad, Persepolis—and then
all the nameless cities, the forgotten and the buried, mere
ruins on hills. Then come the nameless paths, the nameless mountains, and this place we have christened 'the
Happy Valley'.

Every hope is redundant here. There will always be
people who climb Mount Everest and are willing to put
their lives at risk in doing so—a pointless ambition. But
it would be far more pointless to be persuaded to mount
a mule and ride the long, exhausting way back to Abala.

They want to gamble their lives, and they win tenfold on their wager if they return healthy, although the peak of Mount Everest is nothing more than a destination that they have set their sights on to comfort and spur themselves on . . .

But should it matter what we do as long as we use our strength courageously and lead a life without desperation to the end? Isn't it wrong to escape, make a detour and be lost, all of which have led me here to the farthest-flung edge of the world? Wouldn't I have had a good, courageous life if only I had been able to resist sickness and fear? Will I be made to face the consequences just because I had nothing to counter a nameless and agonizing desperation?

Didn't I leave Europe and my homeland for reasons of conscience? It's been two years now; it was important to decide and fight for something even if I wouldn't have chosen this great discord that is tearing nations apart and poisoning people. Being a passive bystander would be unscrupulous, and not possible for me anyway. My desire to fight was even less possible; I felt the role was wrong and I was pushed into it. Yes, I left for reasons of conscience and many envied my freedom and my choice.

Yet, here freedom loses it meaning. I don't want to claim my freedom any longer, I simply want to return and I can't; I can't and I know this.

I awoke today plagued by an inhuman dread. In a dream, I'd wanted to scream and had no voice and when I tried to wake up, and shake off my torturous sleep, dread crept upon me in its place like a dark blanket. I managed to get up and stagger against the tent pole. Outside, fog slid across the twilit fields and from the river, smoke rose; I went to the bank and let myself slip slowly into the water. The cold took my breath away, I was carried upstream for a bit and, at last, I held on fast to an overhanging bush.

Then I lay down once more on my bed and watched the morning light in my tent; a broad, white stream. I was terribly cold. My servant brought me tea, returning soon with the two young Englishmen who had stayed behind with me, the last in the camp.

'We'll take you to Abala tomorrow,' they said.

'It's nothing,' I said, 'I'll be better tomorrow.'

Then I noticed that I really had lost my voice.

Finally, the fever broke out. It was a great relief. I felt it rush through my body and I stretched out and could breathe again. But then it became so fierce that I thought my temples would burst. I prayed, a meaningless prayer that only reached the walls of the tent. Please let it stop, I prayed, but I was convinced that it would never stop. The Englishmen went fishing.

'When we come back, the worst will be over and we'll drink a whisky together,' they said.

I prayed again when they left and believed that I would die of burst temples. Machmud sat the whole time in front of my tent, throwing stones in the river. I told him to go away. 'Someone is coming to see me,' I said. He didn't seem surprised and left without looking back.

I stood up, bent down over the folding table, found a pencil and a few sheets of writing paper. I felt as though I was terribly drunk, swayed back to bed and dropped the paper on the blanket. I lay there, very still, and held my temples with both hands.

When the fever subsided, I began to cry and cried long enough to feel that my head had become quite empty . . .